OWLGLASS

Mr. Harris, Mr. Popghose, Mdes Brock Esq.

WILL NICKLESS

OWLGLASS

ILLUSTRATED BY
THE AUTHOR

THE JOHN DAY COMPANY
NEW YORK

CONTENTS

"Ego te per omne quod datum mortalibus—"

etc.

I

The Law

HARRIS, petrified, hardly daring to breathe, flattened himself yet farther against the bare earth. Overhead, in beautiful clean curves, old Beak and Claws quartered the corner of the field. Harris knew that he was only partially hidden by the spread cabbage leaves. A leg, crawling with tension and seemingly possessed with a life of its own, projected a little beyond the shadow of the leaves, and the rat knew this through his spine. He also knew that to move it meant death. The slightest shift and the owl would spot the movement and he, Harris, would suddenly soar heavenward in its claws. He willed himself to ooze without visible movement farther into the shadow and inwardly cursed the decision that had led him to take to the field, rather than the hedge.

Fact was, he was late. Invited for the second time to

the Club meeting, with of course Meles-Brock in the chair, he had delayed a little, not wishing to appear over-eager in his desire to be with them, and when he had finished the brushing of his coat for the second time he realized that he had cut it rather fine, and that it was no longer a question of his being too early, but on the contrary he would really have to hurry if he was not to call attention to himself by being late. The decision to cut across the middle of the field was natural, certainly, but not sensible. And so here he was, spread-eagled on the ground and awaiting the pounce. Twice more he endured the frightful approach, and then suddenly the owl was gone.

Harris knew this an instant after the owl had flown away. Some extra sense assured him of it, and away with the owl went the fear. Harris stood up and brushed the earth from his coat, so different in mood from the

animal who had lately lain petrified with fear that he might almost have been a different creature. He threaded the rows of cabbages and reached the edge of the field and then broke into a run, and within a couple of minutes he was knocking on Meles-Brock's door.

"Come in, my dear fellow, come in!" said a voice, as he lifted the latch and a blaze of light and warmth enveloped him from the open door; he moved forward down the little passage, pushed the door to behind him, and entered the circle of animals already gathered about the table, or sprawled in the old but comfortable chairs in the badger's parlor.

"Hullo, Harris," said Brock. "Very nice to see you, glad you managed it. But hullo! What's this . . . trouble on the road?"

In helping the rat to take off his coat he noticed bits of earth still clinging to the faded blue cloth of the overcoat, and in the animal's world, the world of danger and sudden death, the question was a natural one.

"Yes, Brock," replied Harris, "old Beak and Claws . . . he spotted me as I was crossing Seven Acre, I'm afraid. I know I ought not to have come that way, but I was a bit late you see. . . ."

"Open field, eh?" said Brock. "Not very sensible, you know, old chap . . . but still, here you are, and none the worse except for the want of a brushdown, and that won't take long. Now what'll you take? There's some pineapple punch just about coming to the brew, or would you care for a drop of something else now? Stuck down on Seven Acre you might have taken a bit of a chill, you know."

"No, I'm all right really, Brock," said Harris, coloring with pleasure at the kindly attention he was receiving from his host. "Perfectly all right, really. . . . I'll have a drop of punch when it's ready, I think . . . there's really no need for anything else you know, not the slightest."

"Well, if you're sure, punch it shall be . . . and here it is. A little more of the nutmeg," said Brock, after tasting it. "Don't you think so, Stoat? Give me the grater."

The badger leaned over the china bowl (it was an old family piece and Brock was rather proud of it, although, being Brock, he never talked about it) and grated a little more of the nut into the brew. "There now, I think that'll do, eh? Now try that, Harris, my dear fellow, get that under your waistcoat and you'll feel a better animal."

The animals were all helped, or helped themselves, to the steaming amber stuff in the bowl, and the general buzz of conversation died down a little as the first glass was sipped, pronounced excellent and drunk off slowly to the dregs. With refilled glasses they returned to their chairs. Brock sat down once more in the old patched armchair that was his usual seat, and from which no animal would have been so rude as to keep him.

"Strange, surely," he said, "old Beak and Claws being about over Seven Acre. He knew we were here tonight. He knew there was a meeting of the Club. The old chap must have forgotten. A nicer owl you wouldn't meet in a day's march, you know. But I fancy he's getting a bit forgetful. Getting old, like the rest of us."

"I think he must be, either that or he's going a bit nutty," said Pointz. "I took him up a bit of something only last Saturday, having more than would keep over, you know, and I don't think he knew me for a moment or two after he'd come down. Shocking shortsighted

he's getting, too. Nice enough, of course, when he recognized me, he was . . . but it was quite awkward for a minute."

The younger animals listened intently to the conversation of their elders. They were learning. Or, rather, from their instinctive depths there slowly welled up the proper interpretation of things that they had to understand or perish. Just as Harris had flattened himself to the ground on the instant, and just as surely as it had never occured to him to shout to the owl and make himself known for a friend (for he had more than a passing acquaintance with old Beak and Claws in the daytime),

so to young Hare and young Harry Vole was coming
the adult code by which they would attempt to preserve
their lives in a sudden crisis. But it was not altogether
easy. It was a very delicately balanced matter indeed
when a larger animal with whom you had talked and
loitered in the morning failed to know you in the dark,
and that animal happened to be feeling hungry.

The general conversation continued to explore the
unusual situation of the owl being over the cabbage
field on so particular a night as that of a club meeting.
An adult owl, knowing his own nature and knowing the
Law which Compels, would, like any other animal,
avoid the possibility of embarrassing his friends by
hunting at the farther limit of his territory. That the
Law would compel him to take his food where he found
it, was known and accepted by each adult without question. But it was odd, to say the least, that old Beak and
Claws had forgotten his social obligation on so important
a night.

"You know, I think," said Popghose, the weasel,
"somebody ought to call on old Beak. There might be a
shocking accident one of these nights, and nobody would
be more sorry than old Beak himself—afterward. We
might easily have lost Harris tonight, you know. You
must have gone to ground pretty well, old chap—old
Beak don't miss much. Before I got to know him I had
a pretty near thing myself one evening. I was young of
course, and it's a long time ago now, it's true. But still
. . . if he is losing his memory, or something. . . ."
Popghose tailed off into silence.

"Yes, that's not a bad idea," said Brock. "One or two
might go, perhaps—a sort of deputation. In quite a
friendly way, of course. Be more important like that,

and more in keeping with old Beak's social standing. Taking him a little something as a present perhaps. Hm-m. Wants thinking about. But it's about time we all had something to eat. It's Mr. Pointz's treat tonight, gentlemen. I was going to get in some of the usual bits and pieces, but Pointz here asked, no begged, to be allowed to give you a little change, didn't you, old fellow? I don't know what it is, but it's in the oven, and if we don't want it to be shriveled to a dead leaf, we'd better get it out and eat it."

The hedgehog blushed and stammered at the acclamation he received. Mink, who was near the door, was told to run into the kitchen for a dishcloth.

"Well, you know, it's nothing much," said Pointz, "and I'm not dead sure how it's turned out, but it's an old family recipe and I've often wanted to try it. I'm afraid the honey was a bit runny. . . ."

He was allowed to get no further. The younger animals burst into a riotous chorus: "The honey was a bit runny! The honey was a bit runny!" and had to be quieted by Brock. "Now, now, quiet, there's good chaps. Come on, let's get it out. Take the cloth, Harry, don't burn yourself now."

It was a sort of covered tart and from it, as it smoked on the table, arose an aroma indescribable. Honey, certainly . . . and bay leaves. A slight suggestion of shrimps and toad-in-the-hole, a stew, blended delightfully with the perfume of apricots!

"What should we take with it, old fellow?" asked Brock. "Nothing much left of the punch in any case, so we'd have to make some more. But what about a jug or two of cider? Would that spoil it?"

The idea of cider spoiling anything with which it

was taken was scouted by all, and Hare was dispatched with the key of the cellar and the largest jug. The tart was eaten to the last crumb, washed down with the cider, and was declared a tremendous success. The hedgehog's permission was asked for it to be added to the Club's recipe book, and so to be eaten on this particular night every successive year, when it would be known from that time forward as Hedge's Honey Treat.

Talk was just breaking out again, when Brock, turning to Harris, said, "Why, old chap, wasn't it to be your story tonight? Your turn, wasn't it? But don't hesitate if you don't feel up to it. It'll keep for the next meeting, you know. . . . How do you feel?"

It had long been the tradition of the Club that the general conversation must be broken into once every meeting, and a story told. The animals took upon themselves the office of storyteller in rotation. It had already been mentioned to Harris that a story would be very welcome if he would oblige at the next meeting, and he had come prepared. He was very conscious of the honor of being asked, and felt that it was in some way a sort of test . . . if he got through properly, and succeeded in really holding their attention, why then, he imagined, they might well vote him in as a full member. And he dearly wanted that to happen. Since he now felt fully recovered from the effects of his grim five minutes under the threat of old Beak, he thought it best not to postpone his opportunity.

"No, really Brock," he said, "I feel perfectly all right . . . as right as rain. It's very nice of you indeed to say I can postpone it, but I don't want to, really. I don't think I'm much of a storyteller, though. You'll all have to excuse a sort of first effort, you know. But I'll do my best if you will allow me."

"Well," said Brock, "that's very nice of you—very plucky, too. Gentlemen," he said, rapping on the table, "pray silence. Silence for Mr. Harris. Mr. Harris will tell the story this evening."

The murmur of conversation ceased. Little groups of animals separated, chairs were drawn up and comfortable positions found. Harris took a gulp from his glass, settled himself deeper into his chair, and hoped he looked less nervous than he felt.

"Gentlemen," he said, "this story is called:

THE STORY OF HOW MY GREAT-GREAT-GRANDFATHER SANG BEFORE QUEEN VICTORIA

"I will, however, if you will allow me, refer to him in the story as my grandfather, and so avoid having to repeat an awful number of great-great's. The full title is such a mouthful every time.

"My family," he began, carefully shutting the lid of

the bowl of his pipe, and sending forward a little cloud
of tobacco smoke, "was first brought into prominence by
the late Lord Melbourne, in the first year of the reign of
Queen Victoria. To be precise it was in the year 1838,
on the third of June—a date that my father ever regarded as a particularly lucky one for his family—that
Lord Melbourne, strolling down St. James's Street,
stopped to watch a performance by my grandfather, and
was in consequence so enraptured by it that he immediately took steps to bring him to the notice of the
young Queen. I should perhaps explain that my grandfather was engaged, not altogether with his consent, as
an actor. It was his task to embellish the rather stale
antics of a Punch and Judy show, and by so doing improve the fortunes of his partner, one Fortunio Scarpia,
whose curbside theatre, in consequence of my grandfather's talent, seldom lacked an audience.

"The statesman who, it will be recalled, was equally
capable of dealing with the most weighty affairs of state
or arranging a garden party, had been asked by the
Queen to advise upon the entertainment of a parcel of
young curates, who were to be received at the Palace
prior to their setting off to the gloom of Darkest Africa.
It was considered, or so my father thought, an advantage for them to be able to tell the Africans about
the Great Queen from firsthand experience; at the same
time, such an honor would nourish a fortitude that
might be useful to them should they be unfortunate
enough to encounter cannibals. With that affability
which is expected, and is only too often the mask of
conscious superiority in a statesman, Lord Melbourne
introduced himself to Scarpia, and told him in the
Queen's name that he must appear in a command per-

formance in the grounds of Buckingham Palace three
days later; that he must remove from his performance
any statements likely to offend the Church and all
vulgarity likely to upset the Queen, and that he must
reserve all political abuse for the Tories. He then, so my
father would say, gave Scarpia two guineas, with particular instruction to provide out of that sum a new suit of
clothes for my grandfather, told the man that any
manual help he might require would be provided by
the Palace footmen, and left after warning him to be
there in attendance well before his time, and to use the
back entrance.

"My grandfather had first fallen in with Fortunio
Scarpia as a fellow passenger. It so happened that they

both selected the same ship in which to travel to England from their native island of Sicily, but owing to some miscalculation on the part of the captain, with whom it appeared the police desired a conversation, the vessel had put to sea hurriedly with little or no food on board for the voyage. Scarpia, as is the way in his profession, had in any case intended to provide his own nourishment, and had thrown into the box with his puppets enough salami, cheese and coarse bread to last him until they landed in England.

"My grandfather, however, was very differently placed. He had relied, as of course was usual, upon what the ship would provide, and when upon a fairly strict examination provisions appeared to be nonexistent, and the only edible thing he had found after a morning's careful search was the rind of half a melon, and that dry, he considered what he should do. He soon discovered Scarpia to be the only other passenger aboard and thought, naturally enough, that by quietly taking up his quarters in the same cabin he might obtain the small quantity of food that would sustain him for the time being.

"He had, however, reckoned without his host. Scarpia locked himself in his cabin and was never out of it throughout the entire voyage. Realizing from the hurried scramble of their departure that the ship would be ill provided, and having paid real money for his passage, he had no intention of sharing his salami with the improvident captain.

"When, on the first day at sea, my grandfather had waited in vain for Scarpia to leave the cabin, he began to be a little worried. He thought at first that perhaps his fellow passenger was feeling ill, being fresh to the sea, and not inclined to risk the movement of the deck.

But since the time would come when Scarpia must sleep, he tightened his belt, ate the remainder of the melon rind, and made what shift he could to wait in patience until night came. When heavy snoring in the now darkened cabin assured him that it was at last safe to move from his hiding place, without further ado he made for the puppet box. What with his hunger and his impatience, he had quite forgotten that the box would be locked. But so it was. The key was in Scarpia's pocket, and Scarpia was sleeping in his clothes.

"My poor grandfather was as far from food as ever, and very soon he began to feel very hungry indeed. He wished he had made the melon rind last a bit longer, but concluding that there must at least be *some* food on the ship somewhere, he left the cabin by the little hole by which he had entered, and made for the deck. The reek of cheap tobacco drew him aft, and in the well near the stern he found the captain, together with the two men and the ship's boy that made the entire crew, engaged in a game of poker. The binnacle lamp provided the necessary light, and my grandfather arrived on the scene just as the captain, scratching his head under his peaked cap, was about to put down his hand. The cards were immediately confronted with a full house from the boy, and with a little grunt the captain pulled his knee from between the spokes of the wheel, motioned to the boy to take control, and bent down to open a box in the well. From this he drew out a sausage, cut about two inches from it with his knife, passed it to the boy, and dropped the heavy lid of the box.

"Gracious heaven, thought my grandfather, they're playing poker for food! Things were as tight as that.

"He hung about for a bit hoping against hope for the

scrap of sausage skin, but the boy ate it himself. In a kind of desperation my poor grandfather wandered forrard again for further search, and his luck brightened a little, for when he returned to the cabin he bore with him a two-inch piece of candle end, and a small piece of chewing tobacco. By eking this out to the uttermost he managed to endure the passing of the next three days, but the smell of the salami when Scarpia opened the box for his meals almost drove him frantic.

"By the morning of the fifth day out, my grandfather had formed a plan by which he might possibly avoid starvation. He waited until midday and when Scarpia was about halfway through his meal, he emerged from his hiding and climbed up to a shelf situated just under the open porthole. The sea lay just below, and if the worst came to the worst he would jump out, and try to scramble up the ship's side again in another place.

"Now while it was his intention to make Scarpia aware of him, he did not want this to take place too suddenly, so having climbed up to the shelf, as I have told, he stood there for a moment or so and waited. He waited until his fellow traveler had his mouth full and had put down his knife to refill his tumbler from the Chianti flask, and at this psychological moment my grandfather gave a little cough. At the instant that Scarpia looked up, he started his performance. He had previously decided that he must avoid any appearance of hurry, so he had chosen for his song the famous piece from *La Boheme*, 'Your Tiny Hand is Frozen,' in complete ignorance, it should be mentioned, that the composer of it was not yet in existence. And so with his heart in his mouth, and his eyes glued to the knife on the table, he started that beautiful aria.

"The first five seconds, of course, were the worst. If the knife was to be thrown at all, it must come at once, and although a hand was stretched out almost automatically to find it, my grandfather had barely reached the second line, 'Let me warm it into life,' before he saw the fingers relax, and watched the whole being of the Sicilian suffer a transformation. The hard eyes melted; the half mouthful was swallowed at a gulp; the right hand quivered and swung out and over to the heart, and leaning back in his chair Scarpia lifted his voice in song, and added a by no means unpleasant baritone to the thinner but exceedingly beautiful tenor of my great-great-grandfather.

"When the song ended my grandfather made a little bow. He explained to Scarpia that he had used the love of music, that lay in the heart of every true Sicilian, as a means of introduction and as a way of calling his fellow islander's attention to the fact that he was starving. He begged a little food.

"Scarpia was by no means an ill-natured man. He too in his time had known hunger, and straightaway he hacked off a lump of salami, backed it with a piece of cheese, and passed it over to my grandfather. But with the cunning of the peasant, he saw immediately what an advantage it would be to him to bind my relative to aid him in his professional capacity. A puppet-size live actor would add immeasurably to his show, and he proposed that they enter into an arrangement. He, Scarpia, would provide food and drink for the voyage, and in return my grandfather must bind himself by indenture to remain with him for, say, three years, to sing and to act as occasion required. He pressed this arrangement with great eagerness, for he knew, although my forebear did not, that the ship was about to put into Valencia, and that at that port both food and cargo were to be taken on board. Had my grandfather known this, he would most certainly have refused the agreement, and when shortly afterward he discovered how he had been tricked, he privately decided that as soon as the opportunity arrived, and it was to his advantage to do so, he would break with the showman who had used his private knowledge in so unfair a manner. However, Scarpia drew up the indenture, it was duly signed by both of them and they both set to work to improve and elaborate the puppet show.

"The ship, old and slow though she was, eventually

reached England, and Scarpia, with his newly recruited tenor, left it at the first port of call, Weymouth. Having assembled the Punch and Judy show and got it upon its wheels, they set off for London. They stopped, of course, at any place likely to prove worthwhile, and although rural England could hardly be expected to appreciate the beauty of my grandfather's voice or the subtleties of his acting, they gathered enough money for their purposes, and enough experience to enable them to fit their program to audiences varying in demand and appreciation. As I have already told you, the first week of June 1838 found them in London, in St. James's Street, and this was the occasion when Lord Melbourne, overwhelmed with delight at my grandfather's rendering of 'On with the Motley,' which was likewise not yet available in the human world, immediately engaged them to appear at Buckingham Palace."

Harris paused, and shook the ash from his pipe into the hearth. The attentive silence of the animals around him made him aware that his story was going well, and he experienced a warming glow of pleasure. Now, he felt, they would elect him a full member of the Club. Brock refilled his glass for him and silently passed it across, and Harris took a refreshing gulp. He put down his pipe on the occasional table beside him, resettled himself in the chair and continued his tale.

"Well," he said, "my father's eyes used to sparkle with pleasure when he told the story of the great success of the visit to Buckingham Palace. They were not the only turn arranged for the entertainment of the young curates. But they were preceded by a long and tedious bout of Morris dancing by village youths and maidens, and since this curious activity is more pleasurable to the participants than to the onlookers, the very appearance of Scarpia's little theatre was enough to banish the tedium and the memory of the gartered swains; so that a little round of applause and a subdued chuckle of anticipated pleasure met my grandfather even before the curtains had fully parted. Scarpia had already experienced the advantage of making no announcement regarding my grandfather, so I can leave to your imagination the astonishment of the audience when they witnessed what they thought to be the performance of a mere doll, but brought to an almost incredible perfection.

"During this part of the show my forebear, I was told, would never utter a sound. All the necessary noises were produced by Scarpia concealed behind the backdrop, as was usual. Imagine, then, the delight when the knockabout of Punch came to its end, and my dear grandfather came on alone and told them in his own voice that he was about to sing! And imagine that beautiful little tenor accompanied by the showman's music from behind, with the baritone added at discretion, in the popular operatic numbers of the day!

"Well . . . it was no wonder that the curates mounted their chairs and waved and shouted. And the Queen was not a whit behind. She was then, of course, very young . . . little more than a girl, I understand. After some of the milk-and-water stuff she had to suffer as entertainment suitable to her station, this must have seemed a rapture indeed. Anyhow she insisted that my great-great-grandfather should be presented. Footmen were sent at a run to get a roll of red carpet, and it was rapidly stretched between the little theatre and the royal chair. The property ladder was rigged and my grandfather descended, crossed the carpet and made his bow. The little

pendant that the Queen pinned on his packet is still a treasured heirloom in one branch of my family, but I myself have never actually seen it. Scarpia too was presented; he made a very decent bow, and was of course in the seventh heaven of delight. Here was success indeed! But it was my great-great-grandfather who was the real idol. The Queen insisted that further performances must be given later that week. Lord Melbourne, her dear Lord Melbourne, must be present with her to see the success of his recommendation. That nobleman had managed to avoid the garden party. Whether the presence of so many curates gathered together in one place had shamed his worldly nature, is not known. But it is certain that upon this first occasion of my grandfather's triumph, the cause of it all was not present.

"Well, the curates departed, and the red carpet was rolled up. The little theatre was housed in the marquee for the time being, Scarpia was accommodated in the servants' hall, and the hero of the day may be seen in the mind's eye trotting alongside his Queen (for he became naturalized a little later), in the most animated conversation, and with her entering the Palace.

"I must pass over the next few days and the further entertainments or I shall never have done. But it was during this great week that my now famous relative decided that he would not return to the life on the road with Scarpia. When the opportunity served he approached Lord Melbourne and told him of the agreement he had made with Scarpia, and of the indentures signed under conditions that were little better than fraud. Lord Melbourne protested that such a contract would not hold in law, and on his return to Westminster he went into the matter with the Attorney General. But, as we already know, there were no witnesses to this infamous arrangement, and so it was difficult to take action. In the end the famous Candle Contract was fixed up, and gave rise to a small chapter in English history. Although the details of it, so far as I know, have never been made public."

Harris paused. Murmurs of delight met him from every corner of the crowded room.

"What a story, my dear fellow!" exclaimed Popghose.

"The Candle Contract, now," said Brock, "I seem to remember something about it, vaguely. Isn't it mentioned by Lytton Strachey somewhere in his life of Queen Victoria?"

"Well, yes," said Harris, "in a way it is. But Strachey knew nothing of the details; indeed he only knew that candles in the Palace were never lighted more than once. But do you fellows really want me to go on? It's getting shockingly late, you know. I could finish the story at some later meeting if you really want to hear the end of it."

The shout of indignation that greeted this assured Harris that there was nothing for it but to continue his story. He took a last puff from his go-to-meeting pipe and carefully laid it down, wriggled himself comfortable in his chair, and said:

"Well, then . . . oh yes, we were about to go into the Candle Contract. But I must go back a bit. At first, after my grandfather's entry into society, quite a few special concerts were given . . . private, of course, Palace affairs, to which only special guests were bidden. Scarpia did not attend these. He was hardly high-tone enough, in any case, and when one remembers that he very seldom washed, and was extremely fond of garlic . . . well. No, Scarpia remained in the servants' hall. But he had no intention of letting my dear late relative out of his indentures. He saw his companion soaring ever higher and well on the way to becoming the pet of society, and he intended hanging on and rising with him.

"The Queen's delight in her new tenor was as firm as ever. But with what might perhaps be described in a lesser person as rather tactless enthusiasm, she decided she would love to hear her favorite in a trio. Who should they have? Blanco was commanded, but unfortunately was ill. Negritto and Bellow were also suffering from some indisposition, and soon it appeared that there were no first-rate singers to be had in all England. There might, perhaps, have been something a little incongruous in my dear great-great-grandfather appearing between two giants, as it were—anyhow, the giants thought so. It wouldn't do—and the Queen was inconsolable. As soon as Lord Melbourne heard of it, he decided that things ought to be put to a better footing . . . perhaps the whole matter was getting a little out of hand. Anyhow, when he heard that the Queen wanted my grandfather put upon the Establishment, Melbourne had to say it would *not* do. It was difficult enough as it was to keep Peel in order, and such a proposal as she was now making would blow the government sky-high. No matter how quietly they went about it, the thing was bound to leak out. Too many people knew of my famous grandfather already. 'No, Ma'am, some other way must be thought of. Scarpia must also be provided for in some way, or you'll never get rid of him, Ma'am, and that wouldn't do at all.'

"It happened a day or two afterward that Lord Melbourne was attending to certain state papers with Her Majesty. He would put forward documents, explain carefully to her their purpose and their probable result, and when all was properly understood and agreed, they would be duly signed and sealed. It was while Lord Melbourne was engaged in this second operation, that of sealing, and was dripping the red wax carefully onto the paper, that he suddenly looked up at the Queen and said, 'What happens, Ma'am, to the used candles?'

" 'The used candles? Whatever do you mean, Lord Melbourne?'

" 'Why, Ma'am, has it ever struck you that there never *is* a used candle? Look around—in these sconces for instance—every candle is a new one—unused. And yet we were in here yesterday for about twenty minutes, if you remember, in the evening. We burned candles for twenty minutes . . . hardly used at all. They must have been changed, Ma'am, for every holder in the room has a new one.'

"It was delightful to hear Her Majesty's laugh. 'How very observant of you, Lord Melbourne! But it is nice, surely, to have new ones, is it not?'

" 'Very nice indeed, Ma'am, very nice. But I would

like to know what happens, I would indeed.'

"He made it his business to find out, too, but it was by no means easy. However, when he knew all he needed to know, he proposed to the Queen that she could obtain her desire to establish my grandfather without any of the fuss that would be bound to occur if he were put on the Establishment. 'Make him Warden, or Steward shall we say, Ma'am, of the used candles. Quite simple. Nothing special needed. We could arrange for part of the proceeds to be given to Scarpia—with certain provisions, of course. He must return to his own country, and so on.'

"And so it was. My great-great-grandfather became Steward of the Spent Candle, and the ultimate profits were enormous. Scarpia was to have a fourth share. Certain interests in the Palace had another fourth, and my forebear had the remainder, one-half of the proceeds. As you may well imagine, the Certain Interests within the Palace were by no means pleased, their share was now cut to a quarter, but they could scarcely complain at losing what in the first place they should never have obtained. And so they said nothing . . . or anyhow nothing in public. Scarpia also kept quiet, and retired a wealthy man to his native Sicily, where he received regularly, every quarter, very nearly enough money to buy up every business in the island, which he very nearly did.

"How my famous relation dealt with his share of the candles is really another story, and is certainly too long for me to dare to attempt to detain you with it. Suffice it to say that when the end came, as of course it did, the factory he had established for processing used candle was the foundation of the family's wealth.

"I said, if you remember, when the end came. But the arrangement lasted for some little time; lasted indeed until after the Queen's marriage. With Peel to back him, for Lord Melbourne's government had fallen, the Prince Consort looked about for things to occupy his time, and among these was the internal economy of the Royal Establishments. Once more the question arose: 'What happens to the used candles?' and you will not be surprised to hear that nobody knew. Nobody. The little arrangement that had worked so beautifully at last came to an end. Had the Prince Consort heard that somewhere on the premises was my great-great-grandfather, now long since forgotten as a singer, but who had made a fortune out of candle ends and was still known and respected by many as a very rich animal, he would not have believed it. I have never heard that the Queen told him anything about it. And perhaps, after all, it was just as well. He was a very practical man, and would have had great difficulty in swallowing such a story."

There was a momentary silence as Harris's story came

to an end, and then every movable object in the room jumped and chattered under the impact of the applause that followed it. He was slapped on the back until he was sore. Brock was overheard to say that the ballot would be taken by all senior members at the next meeting, and nobody felt the slightest doubt that Harris would be a fully privileged member in the near future.

Conversation became general, and the grandfather clock had chimed several times before, in the happiest of spirits, the meeting began to break up. Coats were fetched and wriggled into, and when the younger animals had offered their thanks to Brock and chattered out into the night, Brock held up the departures for a moment and said, "We ought not to break up without settling about the deputation to Beak, you chaps. Who's best to go, d'you think? I fancy three would be about the right number, if it's a deputation from the Club."

Three was agreed upon. One only would make it seem a personal matter, while any more than three would make it appear too official and unfriendly. It was decided that one of these should be Harris himself. He could turn the thing into a sort of joke if he went himself, and of course remind Beak, if he had forgotten it, of what had already occurred. Popghose consented to be the second member, and Brock said that if the meeting agreed, Mink, although not very long among them since he had only recently arrived from foreign parts, had impressed them all with his modesty and his knowledge of the world and was, in Brock's estimate, likely to make a very useful third. Mink thanked them all for their good opinion of him, and said he was quite willing to go with Mr. Harris and Mr. Popghose; but he would not for the world put himself forward, unless they felt quite sure that they really wanted him to go. He was new among them, and there were present several older, and he felt sure, wiser animals than he, who had the advantage of previous acquaintance with Beak. This, of course, was very tactful of Mink, and removed any slight sense of being passed over from the minds of several animals.

So all was happily arranged, and Brock said that if the deputation would drop in on him before they set off to old Beak's place, he would have ready something or other that would break the ice, as it were, and get the conversation going on a friendly footing. He would look around before they came and see what he could find. He'd spent a good deal of time over the years in old Beak's company, and knew his tastes fairly well.

So that was settled, and the little company finally left with Brock's quiet words as he said good-bye to them: "It might be a good idea if you kept together as much as possible; and keep to the hedges . . . keep to the hedges. We don't want to complicate things."

2

The Deputation

"COME in, come in, gentlemen!" said Brock, as he
pulled the little wooden peg from the slat of the
latch. "You're just about the right time, and I was
hoping you wouldn't be too early. We didn't decide on
any particular time last night, did we? But it wouldn't be
any use calling on Beak much before eleven. For the
matter of that," he smiled, "I haven't been up so long
myself . . . we kept it up a bit last night, didn't we? But
come in, come in. I'm just boiling up a drop of coffee,
and I hope you'll join me in a cup." Brock, in dressing
gown and slippers but already neatly washed and shaved,
led the way into the parlor. Harris, Popghose and Mink,
glowing with the brisk walk in the keen air, removed
their caps and followed. Harris, appreciative of the occasion, had brought with him his silver-headed walking
stick, a legacy from a deceased uncle who had spent

33

much of his life in London in a place known as the Ratcliffe Highway, and had only retired to the country in his later years. There was something about the name Ratcliffe Highway that gave Harris a sense of family position. He seldom talked about this, but the stick always reminded him of it, and consequently when he carried it he was apt to assume something of an air. This was not entirely lost upon the other animals, and if an occasional wink was indulged in behind his back, they were careful never to let him see. Harris put the stick very carefully behind the door, pulled the door to after him, and followed his two companions into the parlor.

Brock's coffee service could be described as various and assorted, but the lump sugar was in a real, if worn, cut-glass bowl, and two of the spoons, those in the saucers of Harris and Popghose as was proper, were of silver. There was a jug of hot milk, and letting his guests adjust the mixture to their individual liking, Brock started to remove that slight air of restraint and formality that always hovers over a morning call, even an invited one.

"Now, you fellows," said Brock, "I've thought over the matter of a little present for Beak, and here it is— what d'you think of it? I suggest it's presented from the Club, and not from anyone special. No need to say I'm giving it for the Club. We'll say it's from the Club. Well, what d'you think of it?"

In his open paw was a small leather-covered case. The lid was open and neatly cased within the velvet lining was a curved silver spike like a knife or dagger blade, attached to a silver ring that could be made to open or shut with a snap. The spike was perhaps an inch and a half long. It looked old, and the case, although quite presentable, was rubbed a little about the corners and the velvet was a bit faded. But for all that, it had an air of quality. Engraved along the spike in a copperplate hand were the words *Thunderbolt, April 4th, 1802.*

For a moment or so Brock enjoyed the mystification of his guests, until Popghose, who never cared two hoots that the world might find him ignorant, said, "But what on earth is it, Mel?"

"You may well ask," said Brock. "Funny little thing, isn't it? I've had it for donkey's years, and I'm blessed if I can remember now how I came by it. But I do remember what it is. It's a thing the Others used to fix on the legs of birds for fighting . . . sort of extra spur."

"Well, I'm blessed," said Popghose, "what an idea! What do the words say, Mel?"

"Ah, that I don't know," said Brock simply. "I can read some of the other sort, but that's beyond me. What about you, Harris?"

Popghose, he knew, could not read at all, but Harris had a certain amount of scholarship. Harris would dearly have liked to be able to read it for them, and if concentration upon the fine engraved character of some nineteenth-century craftsman had been enough to solve the problem, Harris would have solved it. But mere concentration being insufficient, he passed the object in politeness to Mink, saying, "No . . . no, I can't exactly make it out. It's an old sort of writing, and I'm like Brock, I can get some of the letters—'O's for instance and the numbers I can read—but I'm afraid it don't make much sense so far as I can get."

Mink took it and quietly read out, "Thunderbolt, April 4th, 1802," turned it over once or twice looking at it with interest, and with a little smile handed it back to Brock.

"Well, I'm blessed . . . does it just like that. Well done, boy. I'd no idea. And now tell us, what does it mean?" asked Brock.

"What do the actual words signify?"

"I don't know for certain," replied Mink, "but at a guess I should say it's just a name and a date. It might have been a prize given after a fight, perhaps. Or a presentation on an anniversary, possibly."

"I suppose it couldn't by any chance *be* a thunderbolt, could it?" asked Popghose. "There are thunderbolts, aren't there? I mean from storms and such. It was said when I was a youngster that the big tree on the common at Eridge was hit by a thunderbolt—although from what I can remember when I saw it last, the damage couldn't have come from such a little thing as that there."

But the general opinion of the meeting was against its being an actual thunderbolt, that Brock's description of his property was the correct one, and that Mink's interpretation was in all likelihood true. They also agreed that it would make a splendid present for old Beak; that it would be a sort of compliment to his prowess in the same field, and that he could not help but be pleased at the offering.

"It's certainly a thing any gentleman could give another gentleman," said Harris, and all agreed it was so. "He could, of course actually *use* it," added Harris, "perhaps when he gets a bit older and not . . ."

He tailed off into silence. The little company were all abruptly switched back into the present reality and the occasion for their meeting. Harris thought of his experience of the night before, and the grim idea of old Beak and Claws adding to his natural equipment in that direction was suddenly seen for what it was, and for a moment or so the four animals were silent.

"Well, now," said Brock, "if you think this little thing will do, you'd best be getting along, don't you think? You ought not to leave it too late. He's almost certain to be there if you make the call now. He breakfasts very late as a general rule, by the time you get there he'll very likely be having his first pipe . . . just the time for a few friends to drop in on him. Off you go now. Come in here again, when you're through, and let me know how it all went."

Coats were put on again. Harris gathered his stick, and with it just the slightest touch of the Ratcliffe Highway as it had molded his imagination, and they set off briskly on their deputation to old Beak and Claws, at the

Bleached Stump, World's End Wood, Rotherside, Sussex.

It was a silent little group that made their way toward the wood. As they walked it struck them in their various ways that they had no real program of approach. What if old Beak was angry? Might he not feel insulted by such a visit and such an errand? Each felt that perhaps they had been rushing things a bit, and that a little more time ought to have been spent in discussing what they were to say. But, perhaps wisely, they did not talk of this openly, and each thought that such apprehension was a private matter and his alone. A quarter of an hour's walking and they were within the wood, and slipping into single file they found the little path of white stones that the rain of years and the walking of little feet had laid bare, and which led to the remains of what was once a considerable tree but was now but a ruin. A ruin, but a picturesque one, for in contrast with the pale grayish-white of the barkless tree, brutally lopped in some long-past storm to a stump about twelve feet high, the deep luxuriant green of ivy, and the twisted ropes of woodbine and creeper combined to make a rather somber but very effective picture.

A more suitable background for old Beak and Claws could scarcely have been imagined. It reminded Harris rather of a white tombstone with an old green coat draped about it, but he put the thought from him as unpleasant. They had quite unconsciously dropped into a pace that was more creeping than walking for the last twenty yards of their journey, and were now arrived at the door. They stood there without speaking or looking at one another, as though they had arrived at the end of something without knowing it, and it wasn't until Popghose noticed the strain on the faces of his two com-

panions that he pulled himself together and forced a
smile. He gave Harris a playful dig, and with the rather
thoughtless remark, "Well, he can't eat us, you know,"
he rapped with the knocker. It was by no means a loud
knock, but to the waiting animals it sounded like the rap
of doom, and they heard it echo in several separate and
distinct tones, as is reached and lingered on the unknown
floors of the strange house before them.

The Hon. Richard William Strix Flammea de Striges,
to give him, for once, his full name, or old Beak and
Claws as he was known to his acquaintances behind his
back, wrapped loosely in the old Paisley shawl that was
his usual morning attire and sitting in his very comfortable old chair, was lingering over a rather protracted

breakfast. Something of a scholar was the Hon. Richard, much given to reading and books, and in evidence of this, propped up before him by the cruet, was a volume entitled *The Anatomy of Melancholy*.

To those of my readers who know that book, it will come as no surprise to learn that the owl was peering at a footnote. As a matter of fact it was the one on page 453, about wine, and the Hon. Richard, defeated in his attempt to decipher very small type in very poor light, was just about to rise from the table to seek his magnifying glass when he heard a knock at his front door. In the very act of rising he paused. Had Mrs. Snipe already gone? He was uncertain. Mrs. Snipe "did" for him, and it was tacitly understood between them that if he did not leave his room immediately after a meal he would be reading, and she need not trouble about him further. She could come in later in the day, as it suited her, and do the necessary clearing up, and since in any case he was always out in the late evening and seldom returned much before dawn, she had plenty of time to see to her own family between the bouts of cleaning and cooking for the Hon. Richard.

When a quiet "Mrs. Snipe?" twice repeated from the landing outside his door failed to produce any result, he realized that Mrs. Snipe had already returned to the rather damp quarters in which she reared her family, and he prepared to descend the long spiral staircase (or rather stairs, for they were built between the outer wall of the tree, and its inside core) and to answer the door himself. He moved very quietly. To move quietly is always an asset to any bird or animal, and the Hon. Richard William had brought the business to the level of an art. When, therefore, he suddenly appeared be-

tween the doorposts of his front door, without the
slightest sound, to the three animals waiting there it
seemed as if he had arrived by some magic, and in their
already worried condition the jump it gave them was
almost painful. He peered at them doubtfully during
their stuttered greetings for some moments before he
recognized them, but on doing so his welcome was so
warm that a sense of relief flooded the little animals.

"Why, surely it's Mr. Harris, is it not? Of course, of
course; and Mr. Popghose. Come in gentlemen, come
in. I'm delighted to see you. And who is this?" he went
on. "I don't think we have met before, have we? No . . .
I'm sure I've not had the pleasure. Pray introduce your
companion, Harris."

So great was the relief of tension in his visitors that
both Harris and Popghose attempted to make the required introduction at once, but when it was sorted out,
and Mink had been properly introduced and had shaken
hands with the owl, they were invited inside, and with
little bows and many an "after you" and the like, they
soon climbed the curious stairs and found themselves
within the room with which my reader is already
acquainted. Chairs were brought forward, coats removed,
Harris carefully putting his stick in a corner where he
would remember it on leaving, while at the same time
searching in his mind for the phrases with which he hoped
to introduce the purpose of their visit in a pleasant and
natural manner.

"You will, gentlemen," said the owl, "please me by
taking a glass of cider, I hope. Wait but a second. . . ."

He produced from a little cupboard in the corner
several bottles, popped them on a tray, and from another
little cupboard he produced glasses, and he was about

to set the collection before them when he remembered cookies. For these he had to leave them for a moment, but was instantly back with Bath Olivers split out onto a salver. A space was cleared among the litter of plates and books on his breakfast table, and in a moment he was back in his chair and ready to dispense hospitality.

With pleasant chatter they ate the Bath Olivers and drank the cider. The warmth of good companionship stole over the little animals, and although the strange house of the owl was no tavern, and only he among them had ever read the great Dr. Johnson, they might well have agreed with that good man, that they were for a few brief moments enjoying what he described as the height of possible felicity. Warmth permeated the body of Harris; Popghose glowed; Mink smiled on the Hon. Richard as though he had known him, not a mere twenty minutes, but all his life.

Within the now tranquil mind of Harris it seemed that discussion about the little business of the previous night, when he had very nearly formed part of the owl's evening meal, was now scarcely worth introducing. But a slight anticipation of how ridiculous it would be to return to Brock and tell him of how they had had a very pleasant morning with the owl but had not seen fit to mention the purpose that had sent them forward, arose in him, and he touched the owl on the shoulder and said, "My dear chap, my dear chap . . . do you know you very nearly gobbled me up last night?"

In the sudden silence that followed, the owl, who was looking at his glass, did not look up. But he nodded, "Yes," he said, "yes . . . but I wasn't sure. D'ye know what saved you? It was your coat. Your blue coat. I caught a glimpse of it at the last moment. But it was a close

thing." Putting his glass on the table he peered at his now silent guests. "The fact is, I'm afraid, and you must excuse me please for introducing so personal a note, but the awkward circumstances you have mentioned compel me to confession. The fact is, my eyes aren't what they were, and I'm very much afraid they're getting worse."

The three animals were about to break in with the feelings of sympathy and pain that they each felt, but the owl with a quick gesture stopped them. "No, please, please, I really must finish what I was going to say . . . if anything can be said in the way of excuse for last evening. I mean about being over Seven Acre. That I should have been elsewhere, and not over Seven Acre at all, is, I'm afraid, indisputable; but really, my dear friends, I can assure you all that I left it until I felt sure the meeting at the Club would have started. You must, I think, have been a little late, my dear Harris, were you not?" Harris nodded. "Yes, yes, but even so that does not excuse me, I know. But the fact is, and I must admit it to you, that I no longer have any certainty regarding my limits farther afield. I hardly need remind anyone here of the difficulties of maintaining territory!"

The sympathetic nods of his hearers reassured him on this point. They all knew the constant pressure of neighbors at the boundaries of forage rights; the constant exertion of moral and physical effort to keep poachers off one's ground; how illness or disability of any sort meant less to eat; and how less to eat meant weakness, and that in turn further withdrawal, until nothing was left in the way of profitable territory. Animals in that condition were forced to leave their ground altogether and make what living they could in the waste places and strips of wilderness that healthy animals disdain to claim.

"So you see," the owl went on, "I can only beg you to accept my growing handicap as an explanation for what must otherwise appear the most disgraceful conduct. My intention is to allow a greater margin of time before commencing my evening activities; and I shall, I can assure you, take the greatest possible care. But danger will be present, I'm afraid; danger will be present."

"What about glasses?" asked Popghose.

"Ah yes," said the owl, "spectacles might do something to alleviate my condition. I have, indeed, been going into the possibility. I use a magnifying glass often for my reading, but my experiments with that instrument in the field are not encouraging. It ties one hand, so to speak, and even so it is difficult to maintain it in focus, if you follow me. Whether the same difficulties would obtain with spectacles I hardly know as yet, but I have been going into the subject, I have been studying the matter."

Harris, although he had perhaps every reason to be dissatisfied with the state of things as explained by the Hon.

Richard, found in the natural fairness of his mind that the owl's situation, which had occasioned his most handsome apology, was most disagreeable. He must either starve or put his friends to considerable risk, but further than that, apparently, he did not see his way to go.

"But come," said the owl suddenly, "we have not yet finished the cider. Harris, now, where's your glass?"

"No, no," said Harris, "we really mustn't. We really must be getting back." He caught Popghose's eye at that moment, and Popghose was patting his pocket, and making curious signs. Harris looked at him in some bewilderment, until it flashed upon him that he still had the Club's gift in his pocket, and that now would be the proper time to make the offering. Refusing once again the owl's offer of more cider, Harris rose to his feet and drew the little leather box from his pocket. Nothing he could say, he began, could lessen the sense of disaster that they all felt awaiting them in the owl's impaired vision. It was, he felt, no exaggeration to say that the Hon. Richard's eyes were in one sense the responsibility of them all, and anyhow he, Harris, with a lively recollection of the events of the previous evening, intended to make them his, so far as he found it possible. But this was for the future. For the moment he, or rather the Club, wanted to make a present, and he begged the owl to be so kind as to receive, as a token of the Club's esteem, this little gift. With that he handed the small leather case to the owl, bowed very neatly, smiled, and sat down again. Popghose and Mink, rising to the occasion, said, "Hear, hear!" gave a little embarrassed clap or two and since they were all about to go, covered their nervousness by looking around for their coats.

The owl was surprised and delighted with their gift.

He said that really it should be he that was giving a present, and not they. This little silver object would remind him, he said, not only of the kindness of the givers, but of the necessity of keeping his natural abilities sharpened to the keenest edge, as must those of Thunderbolt have been in 1802, and that he would ever keep it before him as a token of the triumph of friendship and trust, exhibited in very trying circumstances.

Hands were shaken all around; coats were put on and buttoned up. The three animals followed the owl down the curious stairs around the central core of the tree, noticing the various little doors as they did so and wondering what could be behind them. They stood for a moment or so blinded by the intensity of light in the open again. The Hon. Richard William's door closed quietly behind them as they set off through the wood, to return to Brock and report the ominous news of the owl's failing sight.

3

The Plan

THE table in Brock's parlor, still covered with the remains of a meal, had been pushed back out of the way, and Harris, Popghose and Mink, feeling nicely stuffed and comfortable, were snugly seated before the smoldering logs on the hearth. It was not really cold, but Brock, as he put it, "liked a bit of fire," and there was just enough sharpness in the air outside to excuse the indulgence.

On their return from their visit to old Beak and Claws, Brock had opened his door to them with the greeting, "Now, not a word! You're hungry and so am I. Let's get a bit of something under our waistcoats before we talk. Then we can have it out at our ease and go into it properly, but now I won't hear a word. Now boys, put your things down and come in. It's all ready and only wants eating."

A clean white cloth covered the table, and on the clean white cloth was spread the appetizing invitation of a cold meal. There was a round of sirloin nicely fat at the edges. There was half a cold roast duck, with stuffing. There was a plate of ham. Pickled gherkins filled a tall glass jar with a ground-glass stopper, and a twin jar stood alongside filled with red cabbage. Mango chutney lay in its sweet syrup in a little white dish on which a close observer might have made out the words EUSTON HOTEL in a little oval frame at the edge, with a representation of the great Doric arch that at one time formed the approach to the station. This dish had been a present from Popghose, who had a passion for railways and who from time to time picked up small items connected with them. There was an uncut loaf on a wooden breadboard, which had ears of wheat carved at its edges, and a wedge of cheddar of a golden yellow that had already lost a slice, and showed a fine crumbling at the break. Four half-pints of a tasty drink stood closely together on their own, as though only distantly acknowledging their relationship to the large quart jug, dribbling little beads of froth at its edge, that held cider from the cellar.

With a "Sit down, boys, now, no ceremony," Brock went to the little oven under the fireplace arch, opened it and drew out a large dish heaped with steaming bubble-and-squeak. The pleasant smell of the beef and cabbage, mingling with the faint aroma from the smoldering logs, filled the little parlor with its rich fragrance and whetted four appetites, already razor keen. In the farther recesses of the oven, as was duly revealed a little later, lay an apple tart flanked with lumps of cheese, Yorkshire fashion, and when this in its turn had been attacked, and each animal had protested that he could

eat no more, the refilled jug was put on the hearth in case is might be useful later.

"Washing up now?" inquired Mink.

But Brock, who disliked such chores interfering with and breaking into the contented mood of the gathering, said, "No, Mink, let it wait, old chap . . . I'll see to it later," and squeezing past the edge of the table dropped with a little grunt of repletion into his comfortable old chair. "There," he said, "now all draw up, and tell me all about it. How was old Beak? And how did he take it all? Tobacco, Harris?" He tossed the pouch to Harris, who, it being a visiting day, had with him, in addition to his stick, his best pipe. This pipe, an elaborate affair with a porcelain bowl, a three-piece stem and a tassel, was now slowly filled and carefully lighted, the pouch returned to Brock, and all being done Harris, leaning comfortably back in his chair, began the recital of their morning's adventure with the owl.

"Well," said Brock at last, when he knew as much about the visit and its outcome as his guests, "well, it's fairly plain what we've got to do. Popghose's suggestion of spectacles is, so far as I can see, the only way out. After all, it's not old Beak's fault . . . the poor chap can't help it, and he's got to live, like the rest of us. But glasses, now, they're not things that you can just go and buy like a loaf of bread. Made specially, they are. Made specially to suit particular eyes. Magnifying glasses, of course, you just move about until everything's clear . . . but glasses sit in one place, as it were, and there you are. If they don't suit, they're no good at all, and that's all there is to it."

There was a long silence as the animals sat pondering the problem. They were well aware that the little community that formed the circle of their acquaintance were not without their various skills. Making things, in a certain limited fashion, was not beyond them. They could adapt old things to new uses well enough. And a sort of carpentry, rough and ready it is true, was practiced by several of the animals. But such articles as spectacles were impossible of manufacture or adaptation. These and hundreds of things like them were things of the world of the Others, that world that had always pressed in on them from all sides, was generally a source of danger, but was also, from time to time, actually advantageous. And so, had glasses been a standard article, like a loaf of bread as Brock had said, there would not have been any great difficulty. They would have obtained a pair, somehow or other, from the Others. With a little patience almost anything could be got, provided it was portable. Size, of course, was a problem, but it was about the only one. And in any case, things above a certain size were of no use to them. The useful things were generally small, and so with patience and a sharp lookout, obtainable.

In the end it was Popghose who broke the long silence with a little chuckle, a little chuckle that grew into laughter as his idea developed within his mind, until eventually he sat rocking in his chair and roaring with such merriment that Harris was seriously alarmed for him, and got up to thump him on the back for fear he might choke.

"It's all right, it's all right," Popghose stuttered at last. "Give me a moment and I'll tell you. I believe I've got it." Here he went off into renewed laughter, and spluttered his drink all over the hearth, as he unwisely took a great gulp in order to restore communication.

When he had eventually quietened down sufficiently to make his idea known to them, they gave him their full attention. Not a particularly brainy fellow, Popghose was known and respected as a chap possessed of much sound common sense. Of education, in the ordinary sense of that misused term, he had hardly any and, as the reader may remember, he was unable to read even single words in big capitals. Neither could he add up, multiply, or do simple division. But he had, nevertheless, a system of his own where arithmetic was concerned, and was by no means at a loss to manage the limited applications of this art where they were useful to him. He had a way of repeating vertical strokes and running through them with a crossing stroke, that may on occasion still be found in use in the world of the Others, but he was shy of being seen at this, for he realized that the animals thought him perhaps a little stupid in not mastering the more normal method of counting that most of them found easy enough. His memory was unusually retentive, even for

an animal. He forgot nothing he had once learned, and
on that account alone was considered a valuable member
of society, and was automatically included as a commit-
tee member when anything unusual was being arranged.
Thus he was a founder member of the Club, and
although often silent for long periods, was not considered
unsociable on that account. Unsociability was perhaps
the last thing of which he could have been accused, for
his acquaintance among the various animals was large
and included a sort of friendship with many creatures
that were not ordinarily admitted to be full members
of animal society. Snakes, for instance, were not in general regarded as knowable, but Popghose, was on at
least a nodding familiarity with several. He would also
stop and chat with some of the larger animals, pass the
time of day with cows and horses if the occasion served,
whereas most of his companions would pass them
silently, regarding them as incapable of communication.

It was not, therefore, altogether surprising when
Popghose said plainly and singly the one word "Jackdaws," and looked around about him to see whether
his brilliant idea had been grasped. Jackdaws could perhaps be regarded as on the borderline of the socially
knowable, but if anything a little on the wrong side of
it. They still shared, in the animal world, the reputation
of the sinister, along with crows, ravens and rooks, and
this opinion was known also to be that of the Others.
Therefore when the one word "Jackdaws" reached them,
it was a moment or so before they grasped its full meaning, for they had to conquer the slight prejudice already
in their minds. But one by one they saw what Popghose
had intended them to understand and, as they saw it,
grinned, smiled and finally laughed out aloud.

"Well, I call it positively brilliant," said Brock, "positively brilliant. If there *is* an answer, it's jackdaws. Just go on long enough, of course. No help for it. Bound to work. Only thing is, can you get 'em to do it? True, they're not very busy just now . . . but still, you're about the only chap to put it to them, Popghose. You do actually know one or two of them, don't you? I don't know a soul among them."

Both Harris and Mink also had to admit that, so far as acquaintances went, they had none among jackdaws. If it was to be done, Popghose would have to do it. Popghose nodded. Yes, he knew one or two, but he was afraid it would be a bargaining matter. With animals, now, you might well have got the job done out of good fellowship, but he doubted if that would work with jackdaws. Question was, what would they want? Might want anything, or on the other hand might just refuse to come in at all. Have to find out how they stood with old Beak . . . that might make all the difference. Anyhow he, Popghose, would look in on them tomorrow, put the idea to them, and see what they said. He would report back.

And so the matter was left. They shared out the remains and finished up the cider. Without another word, Mink started gathering from the table the soiled crockery, and together with Harris carried it out into Brock's kitchen. Above the capacious sink was a small hot-water heater, and very nice it looked, brightly shining with its copper pipes polished to a glow. But unfortunately it was not actually connected up with anything in the way of gas or water, and so remained a beautiful, but rather useless gadget. Nor did there seem to the animals to be anything ridiculous in possessing a heater that could not possibly produce hot water. One day it might. One day, if one was patient, the way to make it produce hot water might be discovered. In the meantime one got the hot water from the kettle in the established way, as they were now doing. They washed and dried Brock's china, and carried such of it as was stored in his parlor back into that room, and put the rest carefully away in the kitchen cupboards. Harris took the two pickle forks and put them into the earth outside the kitchen door, to remove the stains of vinegar and the slight taste that clings to steel when used in that liquid. They hung the dishcloths on the little line over the kitchen fire, tidied up a few odds and ends, and went and found their coats.

"Good-bye, my dear fellows," said Brock. "I think, with any luck, we've solved it. Or rather, Popghose has. Don't know what we should do without you, Popghose, old man."

"Ah, we're not out of the wood yet, Mel," said Popghose. "They may not play, you know. But it won't be for the want of trying. . . . I'll see 'em tomorrow. Good-bye Mel, and thank you for everything. I don't know what we should all do without *you*."

Once more Harris, Popghose and Mink set out, but this time for their own homes. Harris swung his stick, looked at his companions and smiled. The falling evening was quiet about them. A little breeze stirred the remaining leaves on a poplar as they passed, and Harris, returning the benediction that the departing sun shed upon them all, said quietly, "What a day, chaps, what a most extraordinary day we've all had!"

4

Popghose Calls on
a Friend

IT was hardly light when, the following morning, Popghose set out to pay a call. He was wearing an old
corduroy jacket and thick moleskin trousers—his working gear, as he called it. He knew he had a bit of rough
climbing in front of him, and had clothed himself
suitably. Ten minutes' brisk walk along the road and he
turned off across the fields, the dew flying in a sparkling
shower before him as he brushed through the long grasses
or took a short cut through tangled undergrowth. The
stout moleskin laughed at brambles and shed the dew like
an oilskin, and he was warm from his walk and perfectly
dry when at length he stood before the bole of a large
chestnut tree that stood sufficiently close to the wall of
a house to overtop its roof, and make in several different
places an excellent ladder up to it.

A moment or two to make sure he was not observed,

and Popghose had nipped quickly into the first crotch of the big tree and was soon climbing from branch to branch until he had reached an overhanging bough that allowed him to drop quietly onto the roof of the house. He made his way along the gutter between the gables until he had reached the base of a big chimney stack, and here, after another look around, he settled down to wait. The chimney pots, which were some eight to ten feet above the waiting animal, suddenly caught the light of the rising sun, and as though this was a signal for which it had been waiting, a jackdaw at once flew in and alighted upon the sunlit edge of the pot. The bird spotted Popghose almost at the moment of touching down, was about to take off again, thought better of it, walked around the pot, and finally stopped and stared.

"Hello, Weasel," it said, "wotcher doin' there?" Popghose, who until that moment had pretended ignorance of the bird's presence, glanced up. He was occupied in taking from one of the pockets of his jacket a little parcel —rather too large for it, and by pretending preoccupation with this task he allowed the nervous jackdaw a moment or two for stocktaking, as it were.

"Why hello, boy, and how do you find yourself this fine morning? It's going to be warm later on," said Popghose when, having finally lugged the packet clear of the lining of the pocket, he found a moment to glance upward again.

The jackdaw, quite still on the edge of the chimney pot, looked down. "Wotcher got there?" he asked.

"Bread and cheese," said Popghose, starting to open the packet. He got out his little jackknife, opened up the piece of bread, and proceeded to spread the butter concealed in a lump within it. Cutting this into several large

chunks, he added a slice of cheese to one of them, grasped it securely, and then looked up and winked at the jackdaw. "Like a bit, boy?" he inquired.

The jackdaw, who had not yet breakfasted and who would, in any case, be unlikely to find anything so appetizing as bread and cheese, said with his beak already watering, "Yes, yes, I would, Weasel."

"Very well," said Popghose, "then you must go an errand for me. When you get back, that"—and here he put on the roof beside him a very decent portion of the bread and cheese—"that will be waiting for you. I want to see Corky . . . can you find him for me and bring him here?"

"Could I have a bit of the cheese now, before I go?" asked the bird.

Popghose appeared to debate the matter for a moment, and then with a quick movement notched off a bit of cheese and spun it into the air toward the expectant bird, who caught it in his beak, turned it over and swallowed it with great satisfaction. Cheese, of which all birds are fond, does not often come the way of jackdaws, and the taste was even nicer than this particular bird remembered. He begged for a further lump before he set out, but Popghose, with a brief "Not on your life—you go and get Corky," stettled down against the chimney to make his own breakfast, and the bird, suddenly fearful that all might be consumed before he returned, left the edge of the pot in a great sweeping dive, and with a "I'll be as quick as I can—don't eat it all, will you?" disappeared from view behind the roof, and a moment or two later reappeared in half-distance, heading for the distant wood.

Popghose, munching the bread and cheese, had every reason to be satisfied with the way his plan was working out. Part one had gone very well; absolutely to program, in fact. Here to these chimney pots a group of jackdaws returned every year to raise their brood. Although this year's brood had long since dispersed and the parent birds had gone back to their quarters in the wood, Popghose knew it to be their habit to return daily to poke about among the chimney pots. They seldom spent longer than a few minutes on these visits, and it was for that reason that Popghose had arrived early and thus made certain of catching the first caller. More often than not, the birds would again make a ceremonial cruise over their hunts toward evening, but at that time of the day would not always alight, and it would then have been difficult if not impossible to attract their attention. Popghose, satisfied with the way things were going, continued to eat his bread and cheese. A sudden thought occurred to him, and thereupon he divided the remainder of his meal into three portions. Two of these he wrapped separately, and put back into his pocket. The remaining one he continued to eat, and when the last crumbs had been brushed from his clothes he fished out a short clay pipe, carefully cleaned out the dottle with his knife, filled the pipe with birds-eye tobacco from a worn sealskin pouch, lighted it, and settled back against the chimney stack with a little grunt of pleasure. The climbing sun now warmed the whole stack, and Popghose slid himself a little sideways to get the whole of his person into the patch of sunlight.

Five minutes, perhaps, passed before a slight commotion above made him aware that his messenger had returned, and a glance upward showed this to be true. Near the youngster, but on another pot and looking down, was another jackdaw, a much older bird, very gray about the head and rather moth-eaten about the rest of his plumage.

Popghose, without moving, said, "Ah, Corky . . . nice to see you. How are you?" and waited. Corky immediately flew down to the roof, followed by the younger bird, who kept at a slight but respectful distance. "Good," said the weasel to his messenger, "you've earned your breakfast . . . here it is," and he slid one of the packets from his pocket over the roof toward the jackdaw. "I've eaten mine," he added, "couldn't wait any longer," and then immediately turned his gaze to Corky. "You will have had breakfast, Corky, yes? If you've not, don't hesitate for a moment . . . look," he added, pulling from his pocket the remaining packet, "I'd saved a bit, just in case I'd roused you too early for you to get anything. Do me the favor of eating it. I wouldn't have asked you to come so early, but I've got an important bit of news that won't improve by keeping. Eat it up, there's a good chap, while I finish my pipe."

Now Corky was no snapper up of odd scraps. Corky was an important bird and had his dignity to maintain. But he was willing enough to unbutton before Popghose; it was merely a matter of getting rid of the young bird who had brought them together.

"Off with you, boy," said Corky. "Mr. Popghose and I have business to discuss." The young bird, with a gulp, seized the remains of his breakfast, muttered apologetically with his mouth full, made the awkward little jump of his tribe, and sailed away again toward the wood. Corky winked at Popghose. "That's better," he said, "where's the grub, old chap?"

"Here you are," replied Popghose, "and as nice a piece of cheese as you'll find. Set to, and I'll leave you to it. What I've got to tell you can wait that much."

When the jackdaw had finished his meal, Popghose folded the piece of paper that had contained it, and replaced it in his pocket. Very useful paper was, and you didn't leave it about all over the place.

"Well now, what is it?" said Corky. "I don't suppose you came all this way to pass the time of day, did you? What's the trouble?"

"The trouble?" said Popghose. "Well, it's old Beak and Claws, he's the trouble, and I'm going around a bit and giving warning to a few friends!"

At the mention of old Beak, Corky sat up. He knew

old Beak well enough. Beak was one of those with whom one kept on nodding terms. He was not a friend like Popghose was, and although he would never have admitted it, he was just a little bit frightened of old Beak, and always saw to it that the jackdaws kept clear of any argument with him. Looking keenly at the weasel, he said, "What's he up to?"

" 'Tisn't that he's up to anything exactly," said Popghose. "The old boy's losing his sight . . . that's the trouble."

There was visible relief on the worn countenance of Corky. He didn't immediately grasp the significance of what he had heard. Doubtless the matter was awkward for the owl, but why the fuss over the loss of a rival? And yet, he thought, why should Popghose, who is no fool, come all this way to tell me about it? The sense of relief faded away entirely as he heard Popghose saying, "Afraid you don't follow, Corky. 'Tisn't that he can't see—you ask Harris, he'll tell you quick enough—it's that he can't distinguish until it's almost too late."

The bird just stared at him, as the new risks that they all ran now flooded in on his mind. Popghose told him the story of Harris in the Seven Acre, and then went on to give him an account of the deputation, and finally of the decision that they had come to that the owl must be provided with glasses.

Corky looked a little more hopeful. "Well," he said, "that's simple enough, surely? Haven't any of you chaps got a pair you don't need? Ah, I see what it is, you haven't, and I've got to get you a pair, have I? That's it, is it? Well, what's that between friends? I'll . . ."

"No, old chap," said Popghose slowly, "you haven't got it yet. You don't understand. Heavens, if it was as

simple as that . . . spectacles, Corky, is all different."
He corrected himself. "Are all different, I mean. No two
pairs alike. Just any old pair is no sort of good at all . . .
might just as well hold a stone up to your eye. Glasses
are all different, and just what sort old Beak needs we
don't know, but"—and here he tapped the astonished
Corky on the shoulder—"we'll just have to go on trying
till we get 'em . . . see what I'm getting at?"

Corky did see and he was thunderstruck. "But it's an
impossibility, Popghose," he said. "How long do you
think the Others would stand that sort of thing? No, no,
it's impossible. Besides, it's not really our cup of tea, you
know. Why should we put our heads . . . we're all pretty
friendly with old Beak. . . . I really don't see. Why, the
Others would make a dead set . . . and where should we
be then? there's already enough fuss made about the
chimneys, heaven knows. We should never get away
with it. There must be some other way, surely."

Popghose slowly shook his head. "There may be
another way, Corky, but we haven't yet thought of it.
And don't think that you all aren't in this. You are, you
know, up to the neck. Think of all the broods in a month
or two. And in any case you're making too much fuss
about the risk. There's none at all if it's tackled sensibly.
One pair at a time. That's all we need get, one pair at a
time. Try 'em. No good. Put 'em back. See? If you put
all your really sensible chaps onto it—not the youngsters
of course, it's no game—but the chaps with a bit of experience and those with something at stake, why, even
if it went on for a week or two, there need be no fuss.
The Others wouldn't even know what was going on if it
was managed properly."

But Corky shook his head. "I don't like it at all," he

said. "It seems to me *we* run all the risk; it's us they'll shoot at. Where do *you* come in? You fellows just sit still, all nicely looked after, and we do all the dirty work."

"Now you just think," said Popghose, "where would you lot have been if we hadn't discovered all this? Look pretty silly in the spring, wouldn't you? For our part, we should not be idle. From time to time, as opportunity arose, we should do what we could. It might even be possible to call the whole thing off in a day or two, with everything settled, if somebody had a bit of luck."

"Well," said Corky at last, "I don't like it, but I'll see what can be done. Have to call a council, of course. May take a day or two; several fellows up country visiting at the moment. I'll send over the boy, 'Yes' or 'No,' as soon as I can get a decision." Shaking his old head, he gazed rather disconsolately into the distance. "Don't like it, don't like it at all. Well, good-bye, Popghose, nice to have seen you anyway. I'll let you know. . . . I'll let you know."

Opening his wings he dropped silently from the roof, and the weasel saw him come into view again at the other side of the house and beat his way slowly toward the wood.

5

The Campaign

THE Rev. Hugh Davidson-Davidson entered his study from the breakfast room. Very warm it was, he thought, for the time of the year, and he went over to the wide casement of the pleasant room, lifted the bar and swung wide the window. The smell of the autumn drifted in to him, and although he always found the departing year a little sad, he had breakfasted on a very nice haddock, followed by a little York ham. The combination of these pleasant foods had settled things to his advantage within his inner man, and although he might not have welcomed the idea, the ham and haddock had arranged between them that his morning should be good. But it was fated not to be so. He gazed, as I have told, out of the window, humming a snatch of music, and thought of the sermon that he was about to compose. The worst was over, for he had decided upon his text. He did not always find it easy to choose a text, but once he had done so the sermon seldom gave him much trouble. If things went well, a round of golf in the afternoon should not be impossible.

He drifted from the window toward his writing table, putting on his spectacles as he did so, and, to prevent any possible break in his train of thought, he accomplished in almost one movement the acts of sitting down, pulling forward his sermon paper, dipping his pen in the ink and writing on the paper these words, "As through a glass darkly." He had scarcely finished the phrase before he paused in some doubt. In what book, and in what verse, did the words occur? The Rev. Hugh had a keen sense of poetry, and it had more than once led him into trouble. He was still apt to grow warm with embarrassment when he thought of the dreadful occasion on which he had referred to the words "The mills of God grind slowly" as a text, only to be told by his hearer that it was a line from a secular poem.

Although perfectly certain that the line he had chosen was from Holy Writ, he was not going to chance it, and he put down his pen, removed his spectacles, and went out through the breakfast room to seek his wife, Elizabeth. Why did he not turn to one of the ordinary sources of reference? Simply because Lizzy was far quicker. She had an uncanny memory for such matters. In a moment he would be supplied with chapter and verse without the necessity of thumbing innumerable leaves of India paper, and have at the same time an opportunity of hearing Lizzy's opinion of the suitability of the text.

When he returned a few minutes later, fortified with certainty and about to sit once again at his table, he was unable to find his spectacles. The room was simply furnished, and having examined the top of the book-shelves, the windowsills and one or two obvious places where spectacles might be expected to lurk, and drawn a blank, he returned once again to the breakfast room. He must have left them there, or if not there, then with his wife in the kitchen.

He did not find them. Two futile hours were spent in the search for glasses that he had had on his very nose that very morning. They were his only pair, but in thinking so he remembered that it was not strictly true. Years and years ago, in youth, he wore pince-nez. He even remembered where he might expect to find them, and after rummaging in a long-discarded collar box in the lumber room, lifted them out in triumph. But, alas, they were somewhat damaged. The little spring that kept the two lenses equally adjusted on the nose was missing, and it was beyond the skill of the Rev. Hugh's somewhat clumsy hands to provide a substitute. Down at his table once more, he tried every possible way he could think of to maintain the glasses in position. He found at last that by throwing up his head in a very affected position, and looking as it were down his nose, the glasses would remain precariously balanced. But the slightest movement on his part that departed from this ridiculous attitude shot the glasses once more onto the blotter, and short of standing with his sermon paper attached to the wall vertically, his pen at the level of his shoulders and his head thrown well back, he could think of no practical way of getting anything upon paper.

He was still hunting for his missing glasses late that evening. Every possible place had been searched again and again. He had even devised a scheme by which he attached a small piece of red paper to all places that had been adequately investigated in order to prevent a wearisome repetition of a hateful round.

Bedtime found him still without his glasses; his sermon unwritten; the round of golf still to play; and his wife a nervous wreck awaiting him as he stamped into the bedroom, to say once again, "But I put them down on to the table for a moment when I came out to ask you about the text. *I know I did!* They can't have flown away." But that, of course, is exactly what they had done.

When, that same morning, Popghose had left one of the many tunnels that led into his little home (for weasels have always considered it advisable to have several

entrances) he was immediately accosted by the young jackdaw, who was awaiting him on a nearby branch. The jackdaw handed Popghose a small folded paper, and on it scrawled in capital letters were the words, YES. STARTING NOW. Popghose looked at the words, but alas, they meant nothing. As the reader already knows, Popghose could not read. "Anything else?" he inquired of the jackdaw. "Did Corky tell you to say anything?"

"No, Weasel," said the bird, "Corky just said to give you this as soon as I found you."

"Well, it's a pity," said Popghose, "for I can't read. Can you read it?"

"What, me, Weasel? No, 'fraid I can't. Shall I nip back and ask Corky what it says? It shouldn't take but ten minutes or so, if you'll wait. Have you got any more cheese, Weasel? I didn't get much this morning, and it's a bit late now, time I get back. . . . I don't suppose I'd find very much about, would I? I've been waiting ages and ages for you to come out, Weasel, honest I have."

"Well, hold on a minute," said Popghose. "I expect I can find you something. Don't know about cheese though." He slipped back into the tunnel and returned a minute or so later with a wedge of apple tart. "Cheese is a bit short, boy, but put this into your stomach . . . it'll keep you going. But you needn't come back. I've got to go out, so I'll find somebody to read it all right. Just say to Corky, 'Popghose thanks you very much, and he'll be seeing you.' O.K. Got that? 'He'll be seeing you.' Well, I'll be getting along."

Nodding to the bird, Popghose set off to find Brock. He must tell Mel anyhow, so he, Mel, might just as well do the reading. But there was no answer to his tap on Brock's door, and after a moment or two's wait he climbed the bank at the back that formed the roof of Brock's house, and went on into the belt of woodland that lay just beyond, as being the most likely place in which to find his friend at that time of day. Having visited several of the possible places in the wood and still drawn a blank, he was about to set off once again when he became aware of noises in the distance, or rather a confusion of noise that was made up of several distinct sounds. There was the faint measured beat of cantering horses, and through it the cry of hounds giving tongue together with the echoes of distant shouting and the notes of a horn. It was the hunt.

Popghose quickly pushed on through the trees to see in which direction they were heading. The sounds had come up to him from the valley and at the other edge of the wood he should be able to catch sight of them and avoid the risk of remaining in their path. Hurrying through the undergrowth to the wood's edge, he skirted it to the right to where he remembered lay a fallen tree. With a bound he was up on the trunk making his way to the highest of the tangled roots now pointing skyward.

Well below him he saw the tiny figures of the hunt to the
left in a line parallel to the wood, while between him
and the winding string of the hunt he was aware of
another moving figure but one coming directly toward
him: it was a fox. The fox appeared to be in no hurry. It
was walking, and hardly bothering to take advantage of
the cover of the small furze bushes that dotted the slope.
When the fox had approached near enough for recognition Popghose got down from the tree and moved forward
to meet him for in the animal now so near he recognized
an old friend and a very famous character thereabouts.
It was Foxy, or as he very much preferred, nay insisted,
on being called, Mr. Williams.

"Good morning, Mr. Williams, good morning. This
is nice! I'd no idea I should have the pleasure of seeing
you this morning. How are you?"

"Why, I'm very well, Mr. Popghose, never been better
—and you? But I need hardly ask, you look as fit as ever
I've seen you."

The meeting was very pleasant to see. The two animals

smiled at each other and sat down for a chat, but the fox, as though suddenly remembering something, got to his feet again and examined the landscape behind him, yawned, turned, and sat down again.

"No, hurry, Mr. Williams?" asked Popghose.

"No, not the slightest," smiled Mr. Williams. "They're safe enough . . . they're on the other side of the line, you know, bless 'em."

"Oh, of course, of course," said Popghose. "Bless me, I'd forgotten the line . . . me, of all animals, forgetting the line."

At that moment, as though to underline the importance of what had been both remembered and forgotten, there drifted up to them, faint and far away, the distant rumbling of a train and the music of its whistle. What Popghose had forgotten, and what Mr. Williams never forgot, was the presence of the single-line railway that meandered through the valley below them. With the hunt on one side of it and he on the other, Mr. Williams was to all intents and purposes safe. He, of course, could cross the line whenever he so chose. But with the perspiring men, horses and hounds, it was quite otherwise. In their eagerness, a few hounds might cross in the absence of the huntsman, but this was unusual and seldom led to any serious trouble—except for the hounds. No, the hunt had to cross by bridges, and the nearest bridge might lie half a mile or more from the point chosen by the fox. And so, when he felt like it, and at a suitably inconvenient place for the hunt, Mr. Williams just crossed the line. Sometimes, when he was in the mood and the scent not too good, he would give them a run for their money, letting them keep him in view, at a reasonable distance of course, giving them the slip when he tired of it. But

now, with the hunt out of the way and peace all about
them, the two animals talked at their ease and made up
their arrears of local gossip, for they had not seen one
another for some little time.

Happily chatting away, Popghose suddenly remembered his mission to Brock and the undeciphered paper.
"Why," he exclaimed, "this is a most providential meeting, Mr. Williams—for me, I mean. I was really looking
out for Brock, you know, when I saw you. I wanted
him to read something for me. I'm afraid I can't read.
Never could master it, except for railway letters, and I
never shall now . . . suppose I'm too old. Would you
mind? There's not many words, actually."

Popghose produced the paper and passed it to the fox,
who very quickly scanned it and explained its meaning.

"There now," said Popghose, "that's splendid, couldn't
be better. If I know anything of Corky, he'll have got 'em
to work already." Popghose then told Mr. Williams the
details of the mission he was engaged on and the matter
of the owl's failing sight, and the fox asked him if there
was anything he could do to help.

"I really don't think there is, at the moment, Mr.
Williams," said Popghose. "Now Corky's got things
moving the next step, I suppose, will be to arrange some
sort of delivery to old Beak. But I'd better see Mel and
Harris about that."

"Ah," said the fox, "and how is old Mel? I'm afraid
I've been a bit remiss lately; what with one thing and
another, I don't seem to have had an evening to myself.
But I really will look in at the Club—next Friday, if I
possibly can. Give my respects to Mel, won't you, and tell
him I'll be along. Now I'd best be getting along myself.
If I know anything about those gentlemen below us"—

here he nodded toward the valley—"they'll be approaching the copse near Stonegate Farm after lunch, and
there's a couple of youngsters down there that I'd better
warn. Well, see you later, Mr. Popghose. Awfully glad
to have run across you. Had a most delightful chat,
haven't we?"

With a smile and a nod Mr. Williams departed along
the edge of the belt of woodland, and Popghose prepared
to re-enter it and make his way back to Brock's. This
time, his little rap at Brock's door was answered, and

within minutes the two animals were closeted together in the parlor. The badger listened carefully to the latest developments, and was amazed and complimentary to Popghose about the rapidity with which he had got things moving.

"Just luck, Mel, happening to get hold of Corky so easily. It was a bit sticky for a time, though, trying to persuade him that we are all in the same boat. I say, Mel, old chap, I bet surprising things are happening now, eh? We'll have to pray that the weather keeps warm like this. If it gets cold, and the Others shut their places up, it'll slow things down, of course; and then it might be difficult to get 'em going again. Corky wasn't exactly enthusiastic about it, and it might be difficult to keep him at it if we don't get some quick results. But what about telling old Beak . . . and no arrangements have been made for actual delivery, you know."

"Well, old fellow," said Brock, "*you've* done *your* share for a bit. I'll go along and see Beak. I should imagine that Corky will get in touch with you again—if they get anything, that is. I'll bet," he added with a little smile, "they won't take 'em in direct to Beak!" Popghose smiled too.

It was later that evening, and almost dark, when Popghose stood once more in the little tunnel by which he had left his home that morning. He was feeling under the mat for his key when his eye caught the glint of the last light shining on something that lay on the doorstep and his paw closed over the object that lay there. He did not know of course, for he had never before seen them, but with his key he was holding the spectacles that the Rev. Hugh Davidson-Davidson had searched for so long and so vainly.

6

In Full Cry

Dr. Felix Richardson had mislaid his glasses. It was most annoying. Morning office appointments were about to start; there were half a dozen or more in the waiting room chatting away nineteen to the dozen, and here he stood, looking like a fool with the empty case in his hand. Now what had he done with them? He pulled himself up . . . a little Sherlock Holmes business was wanted. Now, he had come in through the waiting room, opened the door of the office, put his hat on the peg— yes, there it was—and put his bag down on the chair without opening it. Yes, that bag was on the chair, and still unopened. Then he had pushed up the lower sash of the window . . . and what then? Yes . . . that was it, he had pulled open the drawer of the letter file to get at the specialist's report of old Mrs. Thumper's leg, for he had seen Mrs. Thumper approaching the office from the

High Street and he wanted to read it again before he had to deal with the lady. For that, of course, he had needed his glasses. Had he put them on? No. At that moment, he remembered, the telephone rang, and Miss Cartwright had phoned to say she was delayed by a stupid triviality and would be a few minutes late. To answer the telephone he must have put his glasses down somewhere— on the desk, presumably, for he had only turned away a moment to get at the telephone which was on the other table. Yes, he had put them on the desk, for he now remembered that he had almost knocked over the little jar of flowers that Miss Cartwright had left on his desk the previous day (the doctor was a bachelor), that one or two blobs of water had actually jumped out of the pot— yes, there they were—and he had put down his glasses carefully to avoid the blobs of water. Where, then, were they now? What was the use of all this Sherlock Holmes stuff if it broke down in this ridiculous manner?

During this frustrated pause, Miss Cartwright herself entered, gave the doctor a bright "Good morning, Doctor!" whipped off her coat and hat, and was getting into her uniform when she caught the doctor's eye. "Anything wrong, Doctor? . . . So sorry I'm a few minutes late, but I did ring you, didn't I? It was absolutely maddening . . . Mother had lost her glasses, and she's just not there without them. In the end I told her I really could stay no longer . . . had to leave her to it. Aren't people careless! You know she's absolutely blind without them, and yet I can*not* get her into the habit of putting them back in the case, and putting the case in her pocket!"

She caught the doctor's eye again as she turned. A broad grin spread rapidly over his face. "Your mother and I make a pair," he said. "Just what I've done. I'll swear I put 'em on this desk to answer your call, and now they've vanished. Disappeared into thin air."

Miss Cartwright smiled, and then blushed a little. She was still very young, and she suddenly remembered that she had just made a sweeping condemnation of people who, etc., etc. She hid her embarrassment by turning and joining in the doctor's renewed search, and since the room was quite small, and they had soon lifted and replaced every portable object several times and continually frustrated one another in their feverish movements, the doctor said suddenly, "Look, Miss Cartwright, this is senseless. Will you be good enough to hold the fort, while I run back home? I've got spares. I'll slip out the back way, and you'd better tell 'em outside that I've had an urgent call, but should be back in time to deal with them all before lunch."

And that's what the doctor did. He was back in twenty-five minutes to face his bursting waiting room. He dealt with his patients in his usual kindly way and had forgotten the ridiculous start to his morning until, feeling the unfamiliar frames as his hands removed his spectacles, said, "Good Lord, my glasses! They haven't turned up, I suppose, Miss Cartwright?"

"No, Doctor, I'm afraid they haven't. I'll get along to lunch. I wonder if Mother's found hers. See you again at six, Doctor. Promise I won't be late this evening."

Five minutes later the doctor himself left the office. Pulling the front door to behind him, he was about to step off the narrow village pavement to cross the street when the noise of a car approaching halted him. To his surprise and sudden fear, another gentleman, a little farther down and on the opposite side, also about to cross the street, having apparently not heard nor seen the approaching vehicle. The man was a neighbor. The doctor shouted above the noise of the car, now almost upon them, "Mr. Thomson, stay where you are, stay where you are!" Whether Mr. Thomson heard the words is uncertain, and immaterial, but he heard something and that something was sufficient to keep him halted upon the pavement. Clear of the car, the doctor hurried over to him, to find him still a little hesitant and peering up into his face.

"Why, it's you, Doctor," said Mr. Thomson. "Did you shout? Fact is, old fools like me didn't ought to be out without a nurse. You wouldn't believe it, but I've lost my hearing aid, and I've lost my glasses. How's that for a morning's work, eh?"

It would perhaps be tedious to continue the recital of the strange plague of forgetfulness that had attacked the village. Everywhere it was the same tale, "I had only just that moment put them down," and with the exception of old Mr. Thomson's hearing aid, it was always spectacles that had been put down, only to vanish instantly into nothing.

As the days passed and the list of the purblind grew longer, people began to wonder. There was something mysterious about it. One or two regular customers of the King's Head failed to turn up at that hostelry with their usual punctuality, and Farmer Pettit, who was known to be a heavy drinker, had ordered a crate of ginger beer, instead of his usual three bottles of whiskey, from Miss Postle at the store.

Miss Postle herself, who was among the victims of memory, swore she had seen the devil, or at the very least an imp of darkness. "I'ad put me specs down on the table," said Miss Postle, "to make a cuppa. I'ad filled the pot, and 'ad put it to draw under the cozy, when—may I drop dead!—as I was a-putting my specs on to glance at the mirror . . . just about to raise 'em to me eyes, I was, when a huge black figgur swoops in at the door and seizes 'em . . . right off my very nose, as you might say!" Nobody, of course, believed her. Not even the Rev. Hugh, who at least had what might be called a professional interest in the story, or ought to have had, and who, it will be remembered, had lost his own spectacles at the outbreak of the plague.

"It's just coincidence, my dear," said Mr. Wooley, the schoolmaster, to his wife. "What else could it be? People want wonders, and two or three little happenings

of this sort at about the same time build up and up, until you would imagine that everybody in the county had lost their glasses. And how many had found them again and not mentioned it? Of course, people did lose their glasses, and mathematically it must happen that sometimes several people would lose them on the same day. But depend upon it, there was nothing in it . . . nothing more than that in it, pure coincidence."

Mr. Wooley's own bifocals went the following day. But I will leave the village and return to Brock who, you will remember, was himself going to inform old Beak and Claws of his impending delivery from his embarrassing handicap.

The door having been opened to him, Brock followed the owl up the spiral stairs to the room at the top, and putting his old-fashioned square-topped hat down beside him, sat himself at the invitation of the Hon. Richard in an easy chair, smiled at the owl and pulled out his pipe and tobacco pouch. "May I?" he queried. "You don't mind it in here?"

"Mind it, my dear fellow, why, I'll join you with the utmost pleasure."

The two animals puffed away in contentment and friendship. They talked at ease, and Brock found himself telling the owl of the special reason for his visit: how the animals had decided that if he, Owl, would oblige them by accepting their help, they were almost certain to be able to get spectacles that would suit him, and thus be the means by which unfortunate accidents would be avoided.

The owl was surprised and touched. "It really is too good of you all," he said. "This is real friendship. To think that you should all have bothered about an old

buffer like me!" Of course he would accept their help, and be most grateful. If it escaped the bird that the offer must in some measure have been dictated by the extreme danger in which the little community stood, it is all the more to his credit that he only saw it as an expression of friendship. He listened with delight to the plan they had formed, and offered his cooperation in any way they could think of. "How shall I be able to try them?" he inquired. "Will you bring them here, or shall I collect them somewhere?"

Brock said that they had thought it best to bring the glasses to him. The spectacles would be left on his doorstep, as and when they obtained them. If he would be so good as to leave rejected pairs on the same step, then the animal depositing fresh glasses could collect the rejected ones, and they could then be returned to the Others. And so the matter was left. So pleased and touched was the owl that nothing was too much trouble in order to interest and entertain his guest. Finding that Brock was curious about the microscope, he introduced him to that instrument. To Brock's great wonder he was able to observe the minute creatures that inhabit drops of pond water going about their strange lives. He examined sections of the stalks of flowers and the complicated structure of his own hair, and as his wonder increased so also did his astonishment at old Beak's knowledge.

"No, no, my dear fellow," said the owl, putting aside the quite genuine homage of his guest, "I am but an amateur, a mere amateur. Not that I don't think an amateur has the best of it. It is the right way to wisdom, I fancy. The present trend, or 'drift' is the word I would prefer, in the way of specialization is a shocking mistake. Do you not think so? If one wishes to understand the world, one must stand back from it a little and cast one's eyes over the whole of it, eh? what? Not stand like an insect peering down at the square millimeter under one's nose for the rest of one's life." He glanced at the great clock ticking away solemnly against the wall. Had Brock ever observed the Nebula in Orion? No? Well then, if he would be so good as to follow him to the upper floor, they would be able to rectify that deficiency, if he, Brock, thought it an agreeable way of spending a few minutes.

Brock was all agreement. He was rather uncertain, to say the least of it, what the Great Nebula in Orion might be, but he had no doubts whatever about his desire to be informed. He followed his host up a further stage of the strange spiral stairs and entered the room above which clearly occupied the whole of the circumference of the tree at that level. The roof, or ceiling, had been contrived slightly below the jagged break of the tree, and so was hidden from the outer world. The owl led the way with a lamp, which he extinguished as he deposited it on a small table, and reaching to a small cranked handle above it on the wall, slowly turned it, until above them, with some creaking and goaning, the roof parted and let in the starlight in a slowly widening gap.

"Now," said the owl, "pray excuse me just a moment." It was to a massive object in the center of the room that he now turned, and seating himself in a low chair that was arranged to pivot with the telescope that he was adjusting, he spent the next few moments in finding the Great Nebula in Orion. He then started the clock drive of the instrument, and above its solemn ticking informed Brock that this would cause the telescope to follow the Nebula, and that all he, Brock, had to do was to look through the eyepiece. Brock moved as he was told, seated himself in the low seat from which the owl had arisen, and endeavored in the almost total blackness to find the eyepiece and look into it. This was not so easy, and it seemed to Brock like searching for a black hat in a dark room, but suddenly a slight movement of his head brought his eye central with the eyepiece, and with a gasp of wonder he almost withdrew his eye in astonishment at the sight before him. I shall not attempt to describe the wonder of the Great Nebula in Orion. But if the reader has not already enjoyed it, then I most heartily wish that he may one day share Brock's experience and delight.

Other wonders followed before the owl led his guest

back to the room below, where Brock listened entranced
to his host, who passed from subject to subject as he ex-
pounded the doctrine of the Interconnection of All
Things, and the great profit and wisdom to be derived
from being an amateur of everything. "Knowledge
builds the picture," he said, "but the picture is not
knowledge," a statement that puzzled Brock, who wished
in vain that he could understand it.

The two friends parted that night, each delighted with
the other. If there is one thing that equals a good talker,
and the Hon. Richard was all of that, it is a good listener.
Each had supplied a missing factor to the other, and
when each reached his bed that night, it was with an increased feeling of love for the world, and for its myriads
of living inhabitants.

7

Eureka!

For the next three nights the owl could have been observed in a regular routine. He would descend his stairs each evening as the light was fading, open his front door and peer down at his door step. To avoid mistakes and possible damage, he had put out a couple of shoeboxes, on one of which he had lettered IN, and on the other, OUT. Depositing the previous night's rejects in the OUT box, he would lift the lid and eagerly examine what fresh hopes the IN box might contain. Removing these, he would climb his stairs once again to the observatory at the top, and wind open the roof sufficiently to allow of his exit. This done, he would choose a fresh pair of glasses, and by careful bending of the side pieces, make sure that they would remain in reasonable adjustment. Then four or five steps up a little ladder and he was out on to the roof and away.

He had very carefully selected beforehand an area for experiment, on which he had noticed a colony of ants suffering under some accidental disturbance. These little creatures, he observed, were engaged in continual movement, either in repairing the damage to their home or in removing or replacing their eggs and food stores. Their activities covered perhaps a couple of square yards of ground, but much of their movement was hidden by fallen leaves and rough grass. The owl would float in and soar over this patch, at a height of perhaps twenty feet, and then turning and dropping a foot would repeat the performance. When, after repeated flights, each a little lower than the last, he could detect movement among the ants, he would have arrived at a performance figure for the particular pair of spectacles he was wearing. A few beats of those strangely silent wings and he would be once again on his own rooftop. Entering, he would remove the spectacles, record the performance figure on a label and attach it to the earpiece. This done, he would select another pair and repeat the performance. When each pair of the day's batch had been tested in this manner, he would take the pair with the best performance and set out for an extended test. The patch was now abandoned, and he would repair to the long hedges or the edge of a coppice. Here, the descent of his swift shadow was often the sole prelude to a last and swiftly obliterated flicker within the brain of some small creature.

On the third evening he had the surprise of his life. The regular trial routine had become automatic, and if he could have found a pair that would render his sight as he remembered it at his best, he would have been quite happy. But the third pair on the third evening was a revelation. Not only did it restore his sight to normal, but it actually increased his range. He could now observe the smallest movement at a height before impossible. He made further experiments. The ants had apparently settled their domestic trouble, but the bettles and other small game going about their lawful occasions were watched by the Hon. Richard as though through his magnifying glass, while he was soaring high above the oaks! He desired no more. Excited beyond measure by his new powers, he flew home, pitched all the other glasses into the OUT box, tied it with string, and straightaway flew with it to Brock's. Here he left it in the glimmer of moonlight on Brock's front doorstep, and the word EUREKA, which he had scrawled across the box lid in big capitals, stared up and winked at the smiling moon.

And so it was found there next morning by Brock, when in his dressing gown and slippers he opened his door to take in the paper and the milk. Three pints and a large cream, for that evening was to be a Club night, and there would be company. The box puzzled him, for it was not in accordance with the arrangements made with old Beak, but he carried it into his parlor with the last of the milk and set it upon his table. He stared at the word scrawled across the top but it conveyed nothing to him. Shaking the box produced a chattery tinkling sort of sound, but never having handled spectacles in bulk, the sound, like the word, meant nothing. Brock was a patient animal, and methodical. He still had to wash, shave and dress before he made his breakfast, and after that would be quite time enough to examine the contents of the box.

When at last he had finished his bacon, and a slice of brown bread and butter with marmalade, and had absorbed the contents of three cups and the Personal

column of *The Times*, he pushed the breakfast things
to one side. He put the box on his knee and carefully
untied the string. Removal of the lid exposed the contents, and for a moment he imagined that some mistake
had been made, and that the glasses had been delivered
to him instead of to the owl. There was, however, something about the word EUREKA that vaguely reminded him
of microscopes and Nebula, and his puzzled conclusion
was that old Beak himself had left them on his doorstep,
and if that was so, then in all probability old Beak had
found a pair that suited him and these were the final rejects. This in its turn reminded him that the procuring
of spectacles was, presumably, still going on, and the

sooner it was brought to an end, the better for all concerned—particularly for the jackdaws. Losing no time, he set out straight away to call on Popghose.

Popghose, whose mouth was full of breakfast when he opened the door to Brock, could only smile with his eyes and make gobbling noises, but a moment or two was all that was needed to put that right, and having listened to his friend's tale the weasel agreed to return with him and examine the box.

"Well, old fellow," said Popghose, as he examined the box in his turn, "you're probably right . . . they may well be returned ones, but we don't know, do we? It may be just a mistake of delivery, and old Beak may not yet have seen this lot. What does the word on the lid mean?"

When Brock told him he didn't know, Popghose stared at him. What a strange business this reading was! He could see plainly enough that it wasn't a long word . . . he had seen Brock read much longer ones . . . but these few letters had floored him. But if Brock didn't know, who would? Mink might, but Mink was away on a visit to relations. Suddenly he said, "I know . . . Foxy, Mr. Williams. He said he would be along tonight. I told you, didn't I? Foxy'd know, wouldn't he?"

His faith in the scholarship of Mr. Williams was fully shared by Brock, and that without a particle of jealousy. "Yes, we'll ask Mr. Williams. He'll know, if anybody does. We'd better keep the box here for the time being till we know for sure. But what exactly are the arrangements for returning 'em to the Others?"

Popghose looked blank. "We never made any," he said simply.

"Dear me, dear me," said Brock, "perhaps we ought to have thought of that."

"Yes, by golly, we did ought to have done," agreed Popghose. "It won't be any good asking the jackdaws, either, I'll bet. Oh, my golly! What are we going to do?"

"Well, anyway," said Brock, "I think we ought to stop it now—at least for the present. Even if we are wrong about this lot and old Beak hasn't seen them, it's a nice little bunch for him to try and would keep him busy for a bit. Can you get hold of Corky to stop it, d'ye think?"

"Oh dear, I think we ought to have thought of that, too," replied the weasel. "It's too late this morning to get hold of Corky, I'm afraid. Oh, why didn't I think of a signal or something? They won't come down, you know; jackdaws never do. But there must be some way."

"A signal, a signal," cried Brock. "That's what we'll do. I've got it. Look Popghose, go around and call on everybody and borrow handkerchiefs. As many as we can get. Anything larger would be too much of a nuisance, so we'll just stick to handkerchiefs. We'll stop in a field in which they can't miss it, and we'll spell out the word STOP with 'em. How's that?"

Popghose agreed immediately. He didn't think it could be bettered. "Have you got a bag or something? I shan't be able to get 'em all in my pockets, shall I?"

So Brock found an old kit bag and, better than his word, he joined Popghose in calling on every animal likely to help. In an hour the bag was pretty well stuffed, and the two animals set out to find a suitable place for the signal. After arriving at the house where Popghose had originally arranged to meet Corky, they imagined a line to the distant wood, and set out upon it to find a suitable place. They argued that this line was a regular route for jackdaws coming and going, and with average luck a literate jackdaw should pass that way and spot the signal.

As they walked, the plan began to seem shockingly vague and uncertain, but neither could think of anything better, and so they pushed forward.

Two weary and dusty animals, some two hours later, were sitting in a field; in front of them, spelled out in handkerchiefs, were the words STOP NOW. From time to time birds of all sorts passed over them. Natural curiosity brought some low enough to examine the strange exhibition, but for a very long time no bird landed, or showed anything but a casual interest. And then, suddenly, all was different. Two jackdaws circled over once or twice, and immediately flew off. They returned with a third and repeated the performance. All three then flew off to the distant woods. After what seemed an interminable pause, a single bird was seen to be slowly winging its way toward them.

"Corky!" said Popghose. "I believe it's Corky!"

It was, too. Corky slowly circled, made sure of his facts, and landed very neatly, a few feet away. "Suited, is he?" said Corky, wasting no time. "Thank goodness for that. Couldn't have gone on much longer."

Pöpghose told him what had happened, and how they were not actually sure. They told him of the box with the word on it.

"What word?" said Corky, and when they had explained and pronounced it, Corky smiled. "Well," he said, "none of my lot put that on . . . you can lay to that. That's old Beak for a certainty. In any case, as I say, it can't go on. The Others don't seem to have tumbled completely, only here and there where things were a bit sticky. But it can't last, it can't last. Now I'm going back right away to call it off before there's serious trouble."

"Yes, but, Corky," said Popghose, "what about putting 'em all back—those we don't want, I mean, all but the pair old Beak keeps?"

The outraged jackdaw stared at Popghose as though he could not believe his ears. "Putting them back! You must be mad, Popghose, stark mad, if you imagine we're going through all this risk and trouble once more to return the things . . . well, words fail me. Besides, we don't know now who owns 'em, you don't suppose we put the names and address on 'em, do you? Why, we don't even know where they come from, now! Forget it. If you want to put 'em back, that's your pigeon. But I'm wasting time here, talking nonsense about putting 'em back, with who knows what trouble about to break. I'm off." And as he rose into the air the words came faintly back to them, "Putting 'em back! Putting 'em back!"

Before he was entirely out of hearing Brock called after him, "We are very much obliged for all the trouble you've taken, you know. We couldn't have managed it without you." But the outraged bird, still boiling with indignation at the very idea of repeating the whole performance in reverse, either did not hear him or was resolved to take no notice, for he made no reply.

"Well," said Popghose with a grin, as the two animals busied themselves stowing the handkerchiefs in the kit bag again, "I haven't heard the last of that! Funny things, jackdaws. Old Corky hasn't got what I call a really strong sense of humor, you know. He seemed quite put out at the idea of having to put 'em all back, didn't he?"

The two paused in their collecting and looked at one another and started to laugh, and their laughter grew as they thought of the outraged Corky. Soon they were rolling on the ground in spasms of uncontrollable merriment. "Poor old Corky . . . just boiling, wasn't . . . he?" and away they went again, wiping tears from their eyes, as they roared and roared. They did pull themselves together after a bit, gathered up the remaining handkerchiefs, and set about the return journey.

"Seriously, though," said Brock as they walked, "what exactly are we going to do about getting the spectacles back?"

"Yes, I'm afraid it's one of the things we didn't consider, Mel," answered Popghose. "Still, there must be a way—we'll hit on something, all right. Let's see what Harris thinks about it, shall we? And Foxy, Mr. Williams that is, will be there tonight, remember? We'll ask Mr. Williams as well."

The question was left. The two animals trudged on,

each taking the kit bag for a spell until the other took it from his shoulder, and when at last the final fifty yards was behind them and they stood in front of the weasel's west tunnel, that little animal said, "Look, Mel, come in with me and let's see what we can put together for a meal, will you? With the Club at your place tonight it would be silly to mess your things up, don't you think? I don't feed exactly grand, you know, but I know I'm jolly hungry, and you must be the same. We've had no dinner and it must be past teatime now. Let's put together a sort of high tea, shall we?"

Brock smiled. "That's really a beautiful idea, old boy," he said. "Nothing I'd like better. Sure it won't be putting you out? It would perhaps be a pity to upset my place, now it's so late. We'd have to wash up and so on, and there isn't a lot of time. Yes, it's a grand idea, Popghose, and I'm much obliged to you."

Taking the door key from its hiding place, Popghose opened his little front door. The door opened on to a passage, and the passage led to another door which opened to admit them to the one large circular room that comprised the whole of the weasel's establishment. At first glance the room appeared to consist of nothing but doors. Popghose's obsession with railways had led him to decorate these with the symbols of the various main lines, and one or two of the smaller doors were contrived to represent the rear view of a car that had just entered a tunnel. The other larger doors had copied upon them, with I'm afraid not very much skill, the letters G.W.R. and G.N.R. and so on, all around the room, the letters on the doors being made to coincide with the compass direction. In short, the circular room formed a sort of terminus of all the famous railway lines gathered into one point, but what satisfaction Popghose obtained from this was a private matter known to him alone.

Apart from its curious decoration this circular chamber formed in a way the center of a maze, for many of the doors did lead into further passages that in turn gave access to the outer world. Some of the smaller doors were cupboards, and one was the entrance to the weasel's bedroom. The center of the room was occupied with a large earthenware stove, the chimney of which went straight up through the ceiling. There was a sort of recess on one side of the stove for cooking, the bright brass and copper pots and pans hung in it. The floor of brick, and on it near the stove was a huge willow basket containing wood for burning.

Popghose took down a pair of bellows, dropped some wood onto the embers, and vigorously puffed away until a fine blaze was roaring up the chimney. Happy in his hospitality, he seemed to be able to do three things at once, as he turned to his guest and said, "Now you, my dear chap, sit down and put your feet up. I'll see to all this. While one thing's doing, the other's getting ready you know. You needn't bother about anything. Want to wash? Yes? There's a towel on that peg, and if you go through the Great Western you'll find my bathroom. If you want anything, just shout, but I think there's everything you'll need inside."

Brock disappeared as instructed, and could be heard shortly afterward, blowing and snorting. He was rather a loud washer, and if noise was anything to go by, was removing the dust of the day with great enthusiasm and enjoyment. When he returned, it was to find Popghose smacking down plates on the table, now covered with a checkered cloth; then leaping back to the stove to stir

some eggs sizzling in a pan; bending quickly to spin a weighted skewer that, pivoting across the blaze, was spaced along its length with pieces of steak, bacon and kidney, as well as performing several other operations connected with the making of tea.

Brock was highly amused. "Why, I'd never imagined you were so domestic, Popghose," he said.

"No?" said Popghose, with a twinkle. "Oh, I manage all right. Well, it's ready. Pull a chair up old chap, will you?"

Undoing the little apron that he had around him, Popghose himself was about to sit down when he shot up again, opened the London Brighton & South Coast, and brought out two-thirds of a rich plum cake on a stand covered with a doily, a pot of blackberry jam (home-made) and a jar of meat paste labeled Duck Pâté. "Trying to starve you," he said, glancing at Brock with a grin, while at the same time pulling up his chair to the table.

And so they settled down and ate, and when at last Brock had refused a fifth cup, had turned his chair from the table and was filling his briar, Popghose glanced at the clock and said, "Look, old chap, I don't want to hurry you, but see the time?"

"Five minutes," said Brock. "Five minutes to let it settle. We're all right, nobody ever turns up dead on time, you know. But still, I'll get along in five minutes. But what am I thinking of . . . I'll give you a hand with the washing up before I go."

"You'll do nothing of the sort," said Popghose. "It won't take five minutes when you've gone, and then I can follow you."

The Badger protested, but Popghose was firm. There would doubtless be one or two things Brock would have to do when he got back before the fellows arrived, and by that time Popghose, with others, would be knocking on his door. And when Brock left (by the South Western door this time, that being the one in line with his own home) the evening was already closing down. Popghose washed up and put away, cleaned the frying pan, and went and had a wash. He changed his coat, putting on a new corduroy that had only yesterday come home from the tailors, his best trousers, and his lighter shoes. Putting on his cap, he closed the South Western behind him, and emerged from the little tunnel in time to almost upset Harris, who at that very moment was passing his entrance. With a stream of apology he picked up Harris's stick and hat which had fallen, wiped the hat carefully with his handkerchief and returned them, still apologizing to that animal.

"It's of no consequence, Popghose," said Harris, with perhaps the slightest trace of the Ratcliffe Highway in his manner. "There's no damage. I should have been looking where I was going. But what's the latest news? I don't seem to have seen anybody for days."

As they walked together Popghose told Harris of the latest developments and of the adventures of the day. Soon they had arrived at Brock's door, upon which Harris, taking off one glove and putting it with his stick into his other paw, gave a very decent social-call-sort-of rat-a-tat-tat.

8

Popghose's Story

I T is a proper and honorable custom in clubs to pre-
pare and drink punch, and several members were
busy about this important task when Harris and Popghose were admitted. The club room was Brock's big
parlor, a very large room, paneled in old oak, smoky, dim,
and altogether delightful. A large table, with stick-back
chairs about it, and on which the punch brewers were
operating, had been pushed back to clear the space in
front of the big wood fire blazing upon the open hearth.
Above the high mantelpiece was a large old picture in a
gilt frame, somewhat dull with the grime of years. It was a
half-length portrait of a man, dressed in a fashion now
long out of date. The picture, which had been presented
by old Beak when the Club had been formed, was, he
had told them, of a man named Johnson, and he was, the
owl had said, a sort of patron saint of clubs. Since no one

questioned the knowledge of old Beak, the picture had seemed a valuable acquisition, and they were all rather proud of it.

Several of the deep and comfortable armchairs were already occupied with some of the rather more important members—for there was no nonsense about equality within these walls. The members had all a certain standing based on character, and while each member was concerned that sociability should be the first rule, none questioned the necessity of recognizing differences in importance. Brock, Popghose and Stoat were all founding members. Harris, who had only recently come into the district, was at the Club by invitation. This was his third visit, and he, as we know, was hoping that he was already sufficiently well liked to be offered, by and by, full membership. Mr. Pointz and Squirrel, who were both present, were also full members but neither would have dreamed of taking one of the fireside chairs unless specially invited to do so.

A happy buzz of conversation, now and again broken with laughter, the occasional clink of a glass, for some of the members perferred not to wait for the punch but helped themselves from various bottles upon a side table, showed that the meeting was warming up. Old Beak's spectacles were being discussed on every side, and animals would break away from one small group of talkers to join another, in the hope that additional details of the campaign would be forthcoming. A sudden commotion about the door, followed by cries of welcome, announced the arrival of yet another animal, and in a moment or two the much-hoped-for Foxy, or Mr. Williams as I must of course call him, was among them.

To say that Mr. Williams was popular would be an

understatement. He was much more than that—he was a legend. Quite a number of the younger members had never actually seen him before, for although a founder member, he was often away from the district for long periods, and of late his visits to the Club had been few and far between. Mr. Williams was no longer young, but there was nothing to suggest age in his appearance or bearing. He looked in the pink of condition, and he was —and he would have told you that such was an absolute necessity for any member of his family. Many of the animals present had their stories of traps, shootings and the like, when their activities had infringed on what the Others chose to regard as their rights, their pleasures or their necessities, but the position of Mr. Williams was altogether different. He was in periodic contact with them throughout several months of the year, joining them, as it were, as the most important member of one of their rougher sports—at the leading end of a fox hunt. Thus over the years he acquired talents of survival that few of them could equal, a cunning, both personal and inherited, second to none, while personal bravery was regarded as a matter of course. But these qualities were family virtues, and of necessity possessed in some measure by all foxes. Mr. Williams had in addition personal virtues of his own. He was very generous, and would share or obtain food for others without suggesting the least obligation. Modesty and good humor and the most beautiful manners, together with a fund of good stories and the ability to tell them, made him in their eyes a paragon, as indeed perhaps he was.

Such was the member now came among them, as with twinkling eyes and a glass of punch he was listening with interest to the story of old Beak and Claws. Some of it, as the reader will be aware, was already known to him, but he was now put in touch with the later developments.

"What was that word, Mel," asked Popghose, "the word on the box?"

"Ah, yes," said Brock, "we were going to ask you, Mr. Williams . . . but let me get the box."

He returned with the box of spectacles, and Mr. Williams smiled as he saw the word EUREKA in the scrawled characters on the lid. "Well," he said, "you, my dear Mel, were perfectly right in your guess that it meant that old Beak was now satisfied. It's a foreign word, and roughly translated it could be said to mean "I have it," and of course your guess that no one but old Beak could have written it was like the clever old fellow that you are.

But," he went on, "now that you've got the chief business settled, how are you going to return the rest of the glasses—for I presume you mean to return them?"

They assured him that they did. But how did he think they ought to do it . . . what did he think would be the best way?

"Well," said Mr. Williams, "if I were you, I'd first make sure that you had got them all back from Beak. The box here presumably does not contain all the glasses that have been . . . er . . . offered up, as one might say?" It would be dangerous to return them in dribs and drabs, but when they were certain that they had collected every possible pair he, Mr. Williams, would suggest that perhaps as good a way as any would be to wrap them carefully in a cloth, say, and deposit them one dark night in the porch of the church. They might think of some better place, of course, but that at any rate would do, and there would be very little risk of detection. "Not a word on them, mind," he added, "no letter, or message, or anything of that sort, or they might trace it back." And as for the glasses, the Others would easily sort them out for themselves.

The animals were enormously relieved to hear of so simple a means of returning the glasses. Since they had been obtained individually, they had been trying to think of some similar way of returning them, and the simple idea that the Others would be quite capable of sorting things out for themselves had just not occurred to them.

They all continued to chat happily for a time until checked by a sudden rapping upon the table. "Gentlemen," said Brock, "we must not let our delight in seeing Mr. Williams with us again draw us from our proper

customs. We must have a story." When the clapping and
"Hear, hears" had died down, Brock continued: "I had
thought at first that Mr. Williams himself might oblige
us all, but upon second thought I shall not ask him. It is
enough for tonight that he is among us. No, I want to
call upon my dear friend Popghose. I have spent much
of the day in his company, and I was, before this meeting
tonight, invited to share a meal with him in his own
house. To be with Popghose in his own place is to be reminded of his interest in railway matters, and I hope I
shall not be out of order in suggesting to him that he
might lift the veil, as it were, and let us into at least one
railway secret. But this, of course, is a matter for Popghose alone. We shall listen with interest to any story he
cares to tell us. Mr. Popghose will you oblige the
company?"

Popghose tapped out his pipe on the champagne cork
that he always carried in his pocket for that purpose,
and looking up to Brock with a twinkle, said, "A railway
story, eh? Well, I could tell you dozens . . . and a railway story it shall be. But I warn you it won't start off
like a railway story—it starts off in Persia! Persia, that's
where we English weasels came from originally," said
Popghose, "or so I've always understood."

THE TRUE STORY OF HOW THE GREAT WESTERN RAILWAY GOT ITS BROAD GAUGE

"Of course it's a long time ago now. Hundreds of years.
Hundreds. I know a fair amount about my own particular branch from the stories handed down in the family,
as we all do. Well, as you all know only too well, I'm
nothing of a bookman, or any sort of a scholar, and I'll
admit that very few weasels are. Why, I don't know, but

there it is. Weasels don't take to writing and such. Nor arithmetic. And if the story I'm now about to tell has any point or interest, it'll be partly because weasels are like that . . . no arithmetic. Well, you'll see. And there's another point too, for I think it shows that popular explanations of things aren't always the real ones."

Popghose paused, and felt in the pockets of his yellow waistcoat. "Would you mind, Harris, old chap," he said. "I think I must have left it in my overcoat by the door there . . . my snuffbox, and if I get up I shall disturb you all. Would you mind?" The little oval box of tortoise-shell, with its two circular pans for snuff, was passed over and the weasel helped himself to a generous pinch.

"Much more convenient for telling stories than a pipe. Pass it around, would you, Harris . . . thanks.

"Now where was I? Yes, I was saying that we came originally from Persia. Not that that's really important . . . the real point is that the spreading out and the occupying of new ground had gone pretty far by, say, the year 1000, as the Others reckon it you know, and there was a sizable group of weasels—my immediate fore-fathers—settled in France. Northwest coast actually. Very nice country it is about there, or so I've been told—not been there myself, of course. A lot of sea trading used to go on, though, from there. Quite big ships, as they were then reckoned, used to start out from about there, and it's not surprising that the weasels round about were able to pick up odds and ends, bits of food occasionally, and so on. As the years passed, they got very clever at slipping on board quietly and slipping off again with an armful of whatever was going.

"Well, it was some sixty years or more after the time I mentioned that it became very obvious that some sort of expedition was being arranged by the Others on quite a big scale. More ships than ever . . . and the pickings, of course, accordingly. I've been told that at the time there was nothing you couldn't find—food, wood, rope, any-thing. There was so much of it that it rather led to carelessness. Chaps got over bold and didn't conceal them-selves properly, and there were one or two accidents.

"It was an accident, but not exactly of the sort I just mentioned, that led to my great-great-uncle, or whatever he might have been, for I'm not sure how many genera-tions ago it was, being trapped aboard one of the ships. His name, by the way, was also Popghose, the first name we weasels are aware of. I was named after him. It was, I

understand, one of the largest of the vessels, and he had
gone aboard for sardines . . . salted in those days, they
were, not in oil. Well, he was looking about him before
deciding on any particular box, when he was surprised
by one of the Others hurriedly descending the ladder,*
and naturally he backed into the shadow where he could
keep his weather eye open without being seen. The new
arrival acted rather strangely, or so it seemed to Popghose, for having paused at the foot of the steps and
glanced upward to be certain that he was not followed,

* Editorial Note:
   Popghose must be in error, for there is no doubting his good faith. There
was no decking in ships of the period, which were little more than large
rowing boats carrying a single sail. If it be conceded that the vessel could
have been a "cog" it might tend to prove that this type was in use earlier
than most authorities believe.

he made straight for the pantry, opened the wire door, and emerged a moment later carrying a jar of pickled walnuts. These he proceeded to gobble with the aid of a fork which he had concealed within his jerkin.

"Popghose was outraged. This was plain stealing, and it shocked him deeply. His emotion was such that, heedless of the somewhat delicate nature of his own presence there, he stepped out of the shadow and confronted the man. 'Oh, you naughty rascal,' he said, 'how dare you! What would the captain say if he could see you now? You ought to be ashamed of yourself.'

"The man, who was a well-set-up fellow and lacked nothing either in appearance or manly bearing, recovered after his immediate surprise, put down the pickle jar, and burst into laughter. 'Yes, indeed,' he said, 'what would the captain say! Oh, what would he say!' and again he laughed loud and long. Wiping the tears of mirth from his eyes, he looked at Popghose and straightened his face. 'No, really, I'm very sorry,' he said. 'I ought not to do it. Fact is, I've got a mad passion for the things . . . I can assure you I don't steal anything else. I must try and cure myself of the habit. Would you believe it but I've already this morning had nearly the entire jar! I really must stop it.'

"This unexpected contrition made Popghose rather sorry that he had spoken so sharply. 'Yes, you really ought, you know. One can't be too careful about little habits of that sort. It's not really the few walnuts . . . it's what it may lead to, if you follow me. Forgive me for speaking rather piously, as it were, but I was brought up so strictly that the reproof burst out of me before I was really aware of addressing you.'

"The man, who was obviously quite a gentleman, said that Oh, indeed, he had nothing to forgive, that he really was quite grateful for Popghose's timely reminder, and so on, and in no time at all they were squatting on the ladder together and having a very pleasant chat. When the fellow rose at last to return to the deck, he said, 'Not a word of this, eh?' 'Not to a soul,' said Popghose. 'Cross your heart?' said the man. 'Yes,' replied Popghose, 'cross my heart,' and the man tripped lightly up the ladder while Popghose, remembering his original errand, returned to his examination of the cases of sardines. He found one case almost empty, but it contained enough fish for his immediate wants, and rather than break into a full case my relative contented himself with scrambling into the box and packing his bag from the single layer at the bottom.

"It was while he was so engaged that a sudden rattle of footsteps down the ladder heralded the approach of another sailor, and before Popghose could say Nebuchadnezzar, a full box of fish was dumped smack upon the box in which he was so industriously employed. It was no great task for him to eat his way out through the box, of course, but it took time, and when he emerged and strolled about to investigate a bit, it was only to realize that the ship was at sea. And not alone either. There were dozens of ships around 'em and all going the same way. Sort of fleet, of course, and with the great square sails all set one way, and a nice wind, they were slipping along in grand style.

"Now you must understand that this Popghose, my ancestor, who I think had better be called Popghose I because there're more Popghoses in the story, was something of an original. And indeed, if it's not presuming too much, it has certainly seemed that any member of my family so named has turned out a little in that line. There was one I recall, although a long time after this, that ran a tavern in London, in the City Road I fancy, that became quite famous—although in the usual way detractors tried to pretend that the weasel referred to was some sort of flatiron . . . was there ever such nonsense? However, where was I? Yes, something of a charater, I said. He had the trick of making friends easily. Not only with animals but to some extent with the Others; though heaven knows, that can be very dangerous. Finding himself aboard, there was no question with him but of making the best of it.

"It was while he was thinking of his next move that the topping lift parted. Sort of rope, you know, that holds up the cross beam on which the sail is tied. In the commotion that followed, the swearing and cursing and rushing about of sailors, a little but quite important point was overlooked. It was that the deck end of the topping lift, released suddenly from the weight and tension, whipped forward like a tiger, caught the cook a shocking crack across the back of the neck when he was bending over his charcoal brazier frying sardines, and his subsequent sprawl overturned the brazier. As I say, in the general turmoil nobody noticed it. The cook's station— you could hardly call it a galley in these ships—was right forward in the bow, and his brazier was arranged on a little area of loose bricks. But the spilled charcoal, nicely glowing under the southern breeze, didn't confine itself to the bricks, and in no time at all several little fires were beginning among the odds and ends of ship's gear in the bow. Popghose, of course, wasn't of a size to handle the

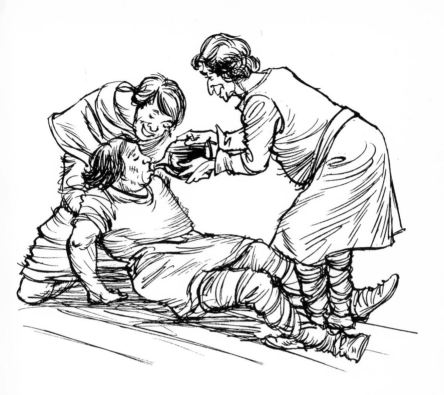

matter himself, but he darted aft and seized hold of the leg wrappings of the first man he saw. Avoiding the blow that most of the Others automatically deal out when surprised by an animal, Popghose, pointed, gesticulated, pulled and in general more or less forced the man to follow him, which he did.

"The fire was easily dealt with at that stage, and the cook was given whatever substitute preceded sal volatile and brought around, and of course Popghose was the hero of the day. The seamen couldn't make enough of him. The yard, which is the name they give to the cross beam that carries the sail, was once again in position and the sail drawing, and the relief felt by all after an escape from a double-barreled accident rapidly turned to affection for the person of my relative, and he was by vote there and then adopted as the ship's mascot, put upon the payroll, and generally made much of.

"They took him along to the captain, and he in turn took him along to an even more important person, who revealed himself, to the astonishment of Popghose, to be none other than the sailor he had last seen below deck stealing pickled walnuts! His new acquaintance, looking up from the chart over which he was poring, recovered from his second surprise that morning, gave Popghose a sly wink, murmured, 'Cross my heart,' and said how charmed he was to receive him, and when the captain had left them together . . . well, you can imagine the rich enjoyment they had in the situation. The liking that already existed between them was now able to flower in the public acknowledgment of their joint existence, and the friendship that grew within the confines of that little ship eventually made history. It is even perhaps the very reason why I am here, and in no other place, telling you this story.

"Well, this new friend, who asked Popghose to call him Bill, explained to him, what indeed was already obvious, that they were on an important expedition. They were to land in England as soon as the wind got 'em there, and endeavor to remain there as its rightful rulers. Bill said he expected he would have to fight for it, for the present occupant of the throne of the lower part of the country maintained that he was the owner . . . a claim hotly contested by Bill, who held on the contrary that Harold, the fellow in possession, had no rights there at all. But the fight, when and if it came to it, would settle all.

"Popghose asked Bill if Harold was much of a fighter,

and Bill said oh yes, he was, very good, and he had some good men too, but he added that he considered it a good omen and a sign of impending victory that he, Popghose, had joined them. They might easily have lost the ship but for Popghose being there, and that fact seemed to indicate that the gods were with them. Popghose asked Bill if he was actually a king at the moment, but Bill said no, the place he ruled in France was only a dukedom, but if the business with Harold came off successfully, he would set up in England for a king. 'Well, that's very nice, Bill,' said Popghose, 'and I think it will come off, though from what you tell me of Harold it might be rather a close thing.'

"Well, it was a close thing, but it did come off, and after the dust had settled down a bit, and the usual kind remarks had been made about the brave dead (I mean Bill's dead of course, Harold's dead were out of luck, they were dead dead, if you understand me, (the serious business of dividing up the land was undertaken. A good many promises had been made before the fleet sailed, and the new owners wasted no time in hurrying off to their claims.

"Not that it was as easy as all that. A fair number of the more important sort of Harold's lot had escaped, and this meant that they got home before anyone was able to stop them. This led to more fighting and sieges and so on, but in the end things did settle down and Bill, suddenly catching sight of Popghose, asked him what he wanted.

" 'What do you mean exactly, Bill?' said Popghose.

" 'Mean!' said Bill. 'Why, land, of course. What would you like? Actually there's not much of the better sort left. It's really staggering how greedy some of them can be, you know. There's Odo's steward, what's-his-name, hardly did anything in the fight but shout, and he's got the nerve to ask for a town with a castle! Greedy lot! But what sort of thing have you got in mind? There's still a bit I've kept back, indeed several bits, pretending it's already gone, you know. Come into the tent.'

"So Bill and Popghose leaned over the long trestle table with the map on it. And Bill pointed out bits here and there that were his for the asking. And Bill put his arm around Popghose, and thanked him for the luck he had brought, and then he added, 'But are you sure, old fellow, that giving you land is going to be any use to you? Would you be able to keep it? It'll be a fight you know, for years yet . . . and not only from the people here, but from my greedy lot. Are you sure land would be of any use? All right while I'm here, of course, but I can't be everywhere, and I'm looking forward to endless trouble . . . and I shall get it!'

"Popghose was silent for a moment or so. He would have liked some land of his own, but he knew it would be next to impossible to hold it against force. 'Look Bill,' he said, 'wouldn't it be possible for you to grant me, say, perpetual hunting and building rights somewhere? Not to give me the land itself, as it were, but to tie down in law somehow that the rights belong to me, and to those that come after me? So that nobody can actually do anything legally to the land without my permission? Is that possible?'

"Not only was it possible, but Bill liked the idea very much. It was in a sort of way just what he had been groping for himself. To make it law. So that was how they worked it out. Bill scrawled a rough oval on the map, and wrote within it, *Popghose—hunting rights in*

*perpetuity. To be fully documented and entered, and all
building rights of any sort or description, with turnpike
rights in perpetuity.* There was some more of it too,
when the lawyers got at it. What it was that Popghose I
actually owned it would be difficult to say, but he certainly owned something!"

There was a pause for a moment and a silence. Popghose tapped his snuffbox, and took a pinch of Blenheim
Mixture which he always kept in the right-hand side of
the tortoiseshell box.

"Well, there it was," he continued, "and when Domesday Book was written a bit later it was all duly entered.
Popghose's rights were legal, but as I said, what they
actually comprised was anybody's guess. But later on Bill
had to return to his dukedom for a time, and Popghose
said good-bye to him and went off to look at his property.
There were miles of it—rather empty, though, but that
suited him well enough. There was woodland and a fine
river in parts of it, and everything in the way of country
that the heart could desire. The Others were pretty
thin on the ground in those days and you could go for
miles and not see one of 'em. It suited Popghose fine. He
lived there in uninterrupted peace for the rest of his
days, and brought up a family there, and they in their
turn brought up families."

Popghose suddenly paused again and then gave a little
laugh. "Golly," he said, "how long I am in coming to
the point! Believe it or not this tale has hardly started!
But I've had to tell you all this so that you would understand how it was that the Great Western Railway had to
adopt a gauge of seven feet! Yes, we've got to skip
hundreds of years and come to a stop in the early nine-
teenth century. You've got to imagine the long and

complicated tangle of the descendants of that first Popghose, still living on the same ground, some of 'em, and
the more intelligent of them grasping from the history
they heard that in some queer way they were the rightful
owners of something or other connected with the land
they lived on. The knowledge passed on from father to
son in the absolutely accurate fashion of us animals.
Nothing in writing, of course, and as I said way back,
weasels are nothing much with the pen. But every eldest
son knew the facts of his forebears, and as the tale grew
in length so the memory stretched to retain it. Golly, the
funny things I could tell you! But no, I must stick closely
to this particular story, for in spite of all appearances
everything I have so far told had a clear and necessary
bearing on what is yet to come. Mel, old chap, might I
have a drink?"

"My dear fellow," exclaimed the badger, "what on
earth are we all thinking of! You must be dying of thirst.
You must blame your tale. . . . But what shall it be? I
think this is a special story and merits a jug of the best
cider . . . but it must go to the vote. All in favor,
please . . . ?"

Brock didn't even trouble to wait for the shout that
followed, but straightaway heaved himself out of his
fireside chair, took the key off the nail, and went in
person to get the precious jug. Lovingly he carried it
into the club room and lovingly he opened it. Little
gurglings as of old and good-humored laughter slipped
with the liquid into each little glass as it was held out
and filled. Popghose, as was the custom and privilege of
the storyteller, drained his glass at a gulp and held it out
for refilling, but one glass only would be the portion of
his hearers, who sipped slowly after the first toast to

Popghose, and made the dregs last. And once again Popghose took up his tale.

"Well, to get on. One evening in the year 1835 a very
respectable gentleman, what the Others call a solicitor,
was reading in his study when he heard a tap on his
window. It was quite dark outside, and he didn't altogether relish the idea of someone, whoever it was, trying
to attract his attention without the formality of ringing
at the front door. While he was musing on this the tap
was repeated, and repeated yet again a moment or so
after, and he realized that he would have to do something about it. In the hall outside he selected his stoutest

walking stick, just in case, opened his front door and
peered out into the dark. He could see nobody. The
house, a pleasant old-fashioned one, was both his private
residence and his office, and it faced directly on to the
main street of what was then a very pleasant little town.
Its name was Reading. Mr. Ironmould, for such was the
solicitor's name, having peered about him and seen nobody, was about to return to his book when a voice that
seemed to issue from a nearby rosebush said, 'Please be
good enough to allow me a few minutes' conversation,
sir. I believe I can interest you.'

"The poor gentleman's hair began to rise upon his
head. He could still see nothing from which the voice
might come, and he began to wonder as he stood there
gripping his stick whether he was not beginning to
suffer from some sort of softening of the brain. The little
figure of Popghose II that then emerged from the rosebush did little to restore his equanimity, but it had the
effect of rooting him to the spot for a moment or two,
and so enabled Popghose to enlarge upon his introductory
sentence. He explained to the astonished solicitor the
difficulties attendant upon a weasel who, having a case,
desired to go to law. The mention of the Law, together
with the urbane and cultivated English of my unknown
relative, did something to restore the solicitor to a more
just appreciation of the unusual circumstances of being
addressed by a small animal, and having gulped a little,
and used a silk handkerchief to remove the cold perspira-
tion from his forehead, he begged the weasel to
accompany him inside.

"They were soon seated together at the desk in the
study, but it was some little time before Popghose was
able to obtain the full professional attention of Mr. Iron-

mould, for that gentleman was still uncertain as to whether he was not dreaming the whole affair. He glanced at the clock in front of him from time to time, and fortunately the continued wearing away of the evening did at last convince him that the interview was actually taking place during his waking hours, and little by little Popghose succeeded in making his companion aware of the nature of the legal business upon which he had called. He inquired of Mr. Ironmould as to whether he was aware of the volume known as the Domesday Book, for between the covers of that compilation, he said, lay the key to his business. At the mention of Domesday Book, Mr. Ironmould sat up. Ancient Rights were his specialty, professionally. They were also his hobby, and he had that very evening, before the arrival of his small visitor, been engaged in the study of the Effect of Lapsed Manorial Right upon Almshouses in Cirencester. I may not have got the title perfectly right, but it was something very like that.

"Anyhow, Popghose told him that he was the legitimate holder, in line direct, of certain rights and privileges by deed of gift from William, Duke of Normandy, King of England, over a very large area in the south, including the towns of Reading, Newbury and Bath. He explained to the solicitor how this had come about; and how as the years had passed successive generations of weasels had seen their rights and privileges overridden, and their title in law unmentioned or neglected and done nothing about it; but he, Popghose II, had decided at last to make a stand.

" 'On what particular ground?' asked Mr. Ironmould.

" 'On the building of the proposed Great Western Railway,' said Popghose.

" 'Phew!' said the solicitor. 'I don't know yet whether you've got a case, but if you have, if you have, my dear sir . . . Dear me! Dear me! The fat will be in the fire!' He then walked over to the bookshelves that lined the wall, and asked Popghose to accompany him he pointed out a row of leather-bound books, 'Domesday, Mr. Popghose—modern copy of course. But it's all there. Can you give me any particulars as to where I should search? No? Well, if it's there, I shall find it. I know my way about that country, Mr. Popghose. Since I presume it might be easier for you to call upon me, rather than the other way about, will you be good enough to look in here, say, this day week? Would that suit you?'

"Well, Popghose said it would suit him very well, and when the week had passed he was met by a very different Mr. Ironmould, a Mr. Ironmould that was beaming with delight at a prospect that began to unfold within his delighted imagination.

" 'Yes, yes, my dear sir,' he said in answer to Popghose's natural inquiry, 'it's all there, all there! Although what it is you've actually rights over, is anybody's guess. Oh, what a case it should be . . . for I take it you are going ahead? Fine! I shall brief Stubben, I think. Quite the best fellow for this sort of thing. D'you remember him in the famous Salt Case—question as to the salt content of the sea in Weymouth Bay—whether it really qualified to be called seawater . . . remember? . . . no, but of course you wouldn't. I was forgetting for a moment. But he really is splendid for this sort of thing. Now, my dear sir. Within the month the Great Western Railway Bill, proposal for, comes before Parliament. You've seen the posters, of course?'

"Popghose said he had indeed, and it was the poster

that had determined his first visit to the solicitor.

" 'Well,' continued Mr. Ironmould, 'I shall get the Member for Reading to put a question. Indeed several questions, and we shall start the ball rolling.'

"Oh, and how that ball did roll! The objections! And the objections to objections! The Railway Company at last saying that there was no real client, and that the whole thing was a put-up job for compensation on imaginary rights, and then the sensation when Stubben, Queen's Counsel, produced Popghose in Court, the existence of whom had been kept dark until the proper dramatic moment. Imagine it! Popghose in the box, fashionably attired in morning coat with a buttonhole, and Stubben Q.C. giving his interpretation of the rights and privileges. It must have been wonderful!

"Wonderful or not, it blew the bottom out of the railway's case, and they saw that they would have to come to terms. There was, of course, no agreement upon the exact interpretation of the Rights and Privileges. The Norman lawyers had made a wonderful job of it, and there might have been no Great Western Railway to this day had not Stubben Q.C. revealed that his client was not interested in compensation. What his client did want was recognition of Interest! 'Accept the fact that my client, Mr. Popghose, *has rights*, and all will be plain sailing,' said Counsel.

"The Railway Company could hardly believe their ears. What! No compensation? Nothing to pay? 'Well,' said Stubben, 'there'll be the Costs, of course'; but apart from that, and the agreement to abide by the stating of Rights by his client, and the acceptance thereof, there was little now to prevent the Railway Company from getting their Bill. Needless to say, they couldn't sign fast

enough. And it was in fact with his pen already dipped
for his signature that Railway President Brunel's eye
suddenly saw the figures that made him start. It was a
little clause in the agreement that stated that the width
of the track was to be seven feet and one-half inch. Seven
feet! Gracious heaven, what was the sense in that? The
standard already established was four feet, eight and a
half inches. He dropped his pen and sought the lawyer,
and the lawyer sought his client. Yes, explained Pop-

ghose, seven feet and one-half inch was the *leap*, for the weasels' standard for measurement of land. What was wrong with it? It was like that before the Conquest. It was a Weasel Law; all land must be measured by *the leap*, and for the same reason it was the standard measurement for *ways* or *tracks*. They had recognized his rights. Very well then, let them at least abide by established customs.

"Well, Brunel fought, he wriggled, he argued; he tried all he knew for the standard track, but Popghose wouldn't yield. Why, he said, this sort of thing was the very point of his going to law at all! Weasels' Rights! Brunel saw that he was beaten. To refuse was to reopen the case, and at this stage they were not in a position to argue against compensation, having already conceded Rights. And so he signed. And the track was to be seven feet and one-half inch, and so it was. To the shareholders and the public it was an engineering decision, of course, and nothing else. It was much safer for the traveling public—and faster. And indeed so it turned out to be."

9

Mr. Williams

I RECORD, in the interest of truth and completeness, that by chance a mole, a stranger in the district, happened to be passing Brock's door at the precise moment that Popghose's story came to its end. The roar of shouting and clapping that followed caused in some sense a repetition of the situation in which Mr. Ironmould had found himself when he heard a voice but could see nothing. But this noise was no voice. It was a thunderstorm issuing from the bowels of the earth, and passed in mole circles later as an unrecorded earthquake.

When the ovation came to its end, it was a rather sad Mr. Williams that looked up at the clock. "I'm really most unhappy having to leave you all," he said, "but I must, Mel, old chap, I really must. I needn't tell you that I would much prefer to remain with you all. . . . I don't often get an evening like this. But I've much to do

that won't wait until tomorrow. You must all forgive me."

Since it was inconceivable that any animal would have left such happy company except under dire necessity, their remarks were only about their own loss, and they did not press him to remain with them. He slipped out very quietly and was gone in a moment, and when the animals returned to their chairs about the fire, had refilled their glasses and settled once again for conversation, Harris said quietly how pleased he had been to have met Mr. Williams. "But Brock," he said, "how did he come by that name? Was it a family one, as it were, or just a personal one?"

"Ah," said Brock, "it's quite a story, that is"—he glanced around the room—"and there're quite a few here tonight that have never heard it, I'll be bound." He paused. "When I first met him," he continued, "he used to be called Foxy. But Lord! That's years and years ago. Just Foxy. But something happened to him, and afterward he always insisted on being called Mr. Williams,

and since he was always very clever at finding more to eat
than he really wanted at the moment, and was quite ready
to pass a meal along to those that needed it more at the
time, so to speak, no one made much trouble about this
little whim of being Mr. Williams."

Brock paused, and tipped a little more from a fat
bottle into his cup, and the clink of glass on glass was
succeeded by a moment's silence, to be broken by a
sudden cracking noise from Squirrel, who had some time
been trying to get to the kernel of a particularly hard-
cased almond, the sort that has a shell twice as thick as
ordinary nuts and consequently can be found lying about
the earths and hides of small animals, waiting for such a
time as this when a squirrel can forget the hurry in
which he ordinarily has to gobble his food. Squirrel,
who was on his best behavior since he had only recently
been elected a full member of the Club, blushed and
muttered an apology; but Brock, lost in his train of
thought about Mr. Williams, took no offense.

"Ah," he went on, "very generous he was to be sure.
And not only about the things he might have cared for
himself. I've known him bring in a couple of mice or so,
or even a few caterpillars in the season, for a sick friend.
And caterpillars weren't his line at all. Oh, no. But I've
known him . . . in the way of friendship."

The little gathering settled themselves into their
chairs. Popghose in the chimney corner silently caught
Brock's eye, and at a nod tossed another log on the fire.
Without the nod even he, a particular crony of Brock's,
would have regarded the action as a liberty, and liberties
were always to be avoided between one animal and
another.

THE STORY OF HOW FOXY BECAME MR. WILLIAMS

"Well," continued Brock, "I think it would be a good thing, and proper if I may say so, if you can all stand a sort of second story, to tell you how he decided on being Mr. Williams. Some of you older ones, of course, know it already . . . known it as long as I have. But with us tonight are several that have never heard it, and besides being a very interesting story, it's got a sort of special idea in it, the idea which Mr. Williams calls the gentleman's agreement. Now you all know about what the Others call fox hunting. It don't interfere with most of us . . . much. We get out of the way, of course, as much as possible on the days, which are always regular, and of course we keep our weather eye open while it's going on, for accidents do happen. But, as I say, it's not our particular concern. It's between foxes and the Others. Now there is, of course, a lot of disagreement about it. Some say, and Mr. Williams is one of them, that the Others being what they are, it's the best arrangement possible. It means, Mr. Williams always says, that at the price of, say a couple of runs a month at the most, in the season, you are left alone for the rest of the time including all the summer. You don't have to worry about shooting, or anyhow not much. Must use your gumption about this, of course, as Mr. Williams would say. There are some of the Others that shoot at anything moving, or even not moving, for the matter of that. But when you've got to know the lay of the land you could reckon, going carefully, on a more peaceful life than most. Take pigeons now. Mr. Williams would say, what sort of life is a pigeon's? . . . Or a rabbit's? But you have got to know the lay of the land. You have got to study the possibilities.

Foxy would say he never took a stroll but what he was on
the lookout for new possibilities. Drains, culverts and
such. In specially good scenting weather, and when it
was likely to continue, he'd go out on the day before the
hunt and lay a bit of trail, and then on the morrow
figure-of-eight it in a special way he has. . . . I've seen
him laughing his head off half a mile up the hill with
the Others all fooling about and shouting and such, way
down below . . . very comic it was.

"Still, I'm getting off the trail myself, now. Where
was I? Yes, well, you see, Mr. Williams was all for the
gentleman's agreement. Given fair ground and only
average luck he reckons to beat them every time. And
mark you, he's right. He could always beat them. Well,
on this particular occasion I'm going to tell you of, Mr.
Williams wasn't on his own ground. Off his own beat, as
it were. He'd gone up toward Mark Cross way to see
about some private business he had to attend to, and
that's a full mile or more from the edge of his ground.
Well, it was a Wednesday, and so the Others were all
out . . . but of course they weren't after Mr. Williams,
no, but as he soon found out, it was a young cousin of
his that was out in front . . . quite a youngster, Mr. Williams said, and not very bright.

"Well, Mr. Williams's business lying where it did,
he had to skirt the edge of the park, and judging by the
wind and the sounds it wouldn't be long before he was in
among them. And right he was. He caught sight of them
rather below him, half a mile away and coming up, and
he moved a bit, so as to be able to intercept the runner
. . . his cousin as it turned out, although of course he
didn't know it then. He stood out from the wood a bit,
right in her line, and joined her as she came by. Young

she was, as I've said, and of course not had much experience, and she'd come through a lot of soft going and
was pretty well covered with mud, a bit out of breath
already, and not in very good shape. Foxy took all this in
at a glance, and without a word, he took up the lead,
and she let him. And his plan came to him as they ran.

"He made uphill, keeping a lookout all the time for
the sort of thing he wanted. He always admitted afterward that he was in luck here, for when he spotted a
likely chance the others weren't yet up, and he was able
to get rid of the girl without their spotting it. It was an
old drain he'd found, and it had got a pretty good scent
of its own. In she popped, and Mr. Williams just waited.
He had to. The Others had to see him, or the girl hadn't
got a chance, drain or no. Scent or no. He said it was a
full minute before they came up and he bore off left at
the very moment they'd spotted him, and as usual they
were all nosing the ground, but he had the luck that one

or two did actually see him. Oh yes, they'd seen him all right, and off he led 'em, up to the left.

"He was fresh, of course, which was more than they were, but as he said he had to deliberately keep the pace down to get 'em bunched and away from the drain. He did it, too. After him they came, not knowing that they had changed foxes, and when he'd got 'em all behind him he speeded up a bit and had a chance to look about him. As you know, it wasn't his country. He didn't know a thing, but what he soon could see, and didn't like, was a ten-foot park wall, of brick at that, a bit to his left, and endless. He gave that up without a second thought, and eased off to the right, took a fence of two and was soon coming down the other side of the hill. It was steeper this side, and not much of it, for before he was able to take stock of the position he was over a wall around a market garden, and had landed smack into a village street.

"Well, as Foxy told me, this was no sort of good at all. Comes of not knowing the ground. Left or right? He went left, going flat out now and no playing about. Tidy village it was, he said, nicely kept, and when he saw gates ahead of him, he realized what he'd done. He'd got back to the park wall, but here at least was a gate. One of those big things, gold and iron and all that sort of thing. A lodge, probably empty, but of course he didn't know. Shut, the gate was, but plenty of room between bars, and he was through it and into the drive in a shake. At the same moment he heard the noises behind him and the yelping . . . the hunt was coming up through the village." Brock paused, and tipped out a little more from the bottle into his cup.

"Anything left in the bowl, Popghose? Do help yourselves, there's a good chaps. Make some more if you like. There's a bottle in the cupboard just behind you, and the kettle's still singing. And you'd better have another lemon and sugar. Run to the kitchen, Stoaty, there's a good fellow, and bring 'em in."

The little animals busied themselves and they soon had some more punch a-brewing. Brock, with a "Heavens, what am I thinking of!" heaved himself out of his chair, and went to the iron door over the fireplace. He took from the oven a large pudding basin covered with a plate, as well as a little pile of plates set to warm in the back of the oven. "Here now," he said, "don't burn yourselves." Layered in slices in the pudding basin were mushrooms on toast on which grated cheese had been sprinkled, with butter soaked so through and through the bread that the whole contents of the basin had become a sort of pudding.

Gingerly the animals put their paws in the basin and ladled out the hot slices, and soon munching, and sipping the newly made punch, they were urging a continuation of the story. "And what happened, Brock? What did he do? How did he get away?"

Brock filled his pipe. "Well, if you're all finished eating, I'll tell you the rest of it," he said. "Popghose, some baccy? Good, catch." Glad of a change from his birds-eye, Popghose filled his pipe from the badger's pouch and lighted it, and they all settled into their seats again and Brock continued his story.

"Let me see, where were we? Yes, Mr. Williams was through into the drive, wasn't he? Yes, that was it. Well, as he said, it wasn't much good running. It was a case

of thinking before running . . . the running would come all right when he'd got some idea where to make for. He slipped into the shrubbery at the side of the drive and made toward the house. Big place it was, low and gray and old. Outbuildings at the sides. He could smell stables behind somewhere, and of course the scent of dogs everywhere. All sorts of dogs, but not hounds. So that told him that hounds were not kept there, and although he could hear them giving tongue away at the great gate, with the whips a-going, and the Others all a-talking and shouting away, he doubted whether they'd be let in, and wondered whether with luck this might not be the end of the run, and in a little while and watching his step he might not be able to slip into the park at the back and so find his way around and home again.

"All this calculation was brought to a sudden end by

his hearing runnings steps behind him, and a voice shouting, 'Through the gate d'you say?' together with the rustle of leaves and the snapping of twigs, as the running feet took to the shrubbery. Having no option but to get on, he did so, and all might have been well but for the sudden arrival of a bunch of the Others, of both sorts, making in a hurry for the great gate, so as to miss none of the excitement.

"They saw him, of course, in flat full view he was, in a yard. Gates, doors, walls and whatnot all around, and the excited mob all a-shouting: ' 'Ere 'e is! Come on! This way, Mr. Williams! 'Ere 'e is, sir, 'ere's the fox, sir!'

"Well, clever or no—and he *is* clever, make no mistake about that—there was precious little he could do. Just keep his head to the last, and see what chance might offer him. He made for the opening of the largest shed in the yard, and to get to it he had to dash right through the yelling mob. Big shed it was, as I said, and dark inside after the daylight, and stacked pretty well from floor to rafters with firewood, logs, cut stuff and twiggery. Lord! he thought. Still a chance! and he plunged into openings in the big stuff—pieces four foot long or so, loosely stacked against the side wall. Right inside he wriggled . . . it would take 'em some time to move all that lot, he knew. But he didn't have to wait, for when he got to the wall right at the back, there in front of his nose was an opening. A fireplace, empty. He was in that fireplace and up that flue in a shake. It was just narrow enough, and just wide enough, if you understand me, to be climbable. A bit more or a bit less, and he couldn't have done it. He came out at the chimney and jumped down to the roof.

"Now, you youngsters, you'll see now that Foxy has brains, and could use 'em. You see, he now had a choice of action. He could run over the roofs, for they were all joined up one to the other at different levels, as I said, in a higgledy-piggledy manner, and he could find an easy place and scramble down to the ground again, or he could stay where he was, playing a sort of hide-and-seek, in among the hip roofs and chimney stacks, and keeping out of sight of the ground.

"By now, of course, the whole place below was a mass of the Others. The hunt, too, had spread itself around the building and one or two of the hounds, on leash, were being led into the yard. A terrier was put into the wood pile, but not understanding his impatient barking when he reached the fireplace, they left him there and started to remove the wood. Foxy followed all this by the sounds, and he admitted afterward that he didn't much like what he heard. To get back to the ground was easy . . . but what chance had he then? As soon as the Others discovered the chimney they'd tumble to where he was, and be up after him with the terrier. They wouldn't come up the chimney, of course, but Foxy knew there were other ways to get onto roofs. They've got little trapdoors from inside. Then the idea came to him that having come up one chimney, he could go down another. And that's what he did. He would play hide-and-seek, not only forward and backward, but up and down as well! There were so many chimneys that he reckoned he might be able to play for quite a time—until they got tired of it, in fact, and gave him a chance to get right away.

"However, as Foxy said when he told me, it didn't work out quite like that. His experience of chimneys was limited to the one he had scrambled up, and when, having chosen a pot some distance away, he had climbed into it, it was only to realize that the shaft was very much wider than the first one, so that scrambling down was quite impossible, and he had no option but to let go and chance it, which he did. He landed, squarely enough, into another empty fireplace, behind a fireback, but a very much larger fireplace than the one in the woodshed, and he was in a room. The door was shut. The windows were large, and made of many little pieces of glass. And they were also shut. Mr. Williams was a prisoner, for there was no scrambling up that wide hole by which he had entered.

"It looked to him, he said, very much like the end. Naturally he examined the room. There might be some other way. The room was mostly books in shelves. There was a glass-fronted gun cupboard with guns in it, a table with papers and various things on it, and a chair or two. On the floor was a nice carpet, and the floor itself was of polished shiny wood in little blocks. But there was no way out. In the house all was silence. He could still hear the excitement outside, but after a bit it didn't sound so urgent, and when an hour had passed, it ceased entirely. The Others, he realized, had assumed that he had got away, scrambled down the wall and streaked through the park. He wished he had. There was nothing to eat in the room. There was nothing he could do in the way of escape, so he sat down and set to work to get himself clean, which having done, he lay down on the carpet in front of the open fireplace.

"The light faded from the windows and it became quite dark. Small sounds would occasionally filter up from the big house. Having nothing whatever to do, and, as he afterward said, in spite of all he could do to prevent it, he must have fallen asleep. Danger, of course, would have aroused him immediately. But what danger was there? None. And he slept for exactly four hours, and of course knew the time to a tee when he was suddenly awakened by a click sound and a blaze of light."

There was a subdued murmur from the assembled animals as Brock ceased speaking. A little gasp or two, and a shifting and wriggling in chairs. But no one spoke, and Brock, after lighting his pipe again and taking a puff or two, continued his tale.

"Standing in the open doorway was a tall, middle-aged man with a book under his arm and the fingers of his hand between the pages of the book. His other hand was on the knob of the door. There was a pipe between his teeth, and he stood stock still and looking down at Foxy. Foxy, awake in an instant, knew him. It was the man they had called Mr. Williams that morning in the yard. Foxy quietly sat up and looked at Mr. Williams. They looked at one another for perhaps ten seconds, and

neither moved. The man took his hand from the door and inclined his body slowly toward Foxy, and still looking at him said, 'Will you be good enough to follow me? I will show you out.' And that was all. Foxy understood perfectly, and went down the long corridors of that old house quietly at the heels of Mr. Williams. A turn or two and they descended a few stairs, and there in front of them was a door, which Mr. Williams opened very quietly. Again quietly, and with the door wide open, he inclined slightly toward Foxy, and for perhaps five seconds again they stared at one another. And then Foxy turned and was out under the starlight, and he heard the door quietly close behind him. And," went on Brock, "that's all. That's absolutely all.

"I saw him a day or two after all this happened and he told me the whole thing just as I now tell you. He told me too that he had changed his name, and was now going to be called Mr. Williams. Not all the animals understood this and there was a certain amount of quiet fun behind Foxy's back about it. But I understood it all right. And as I said at the beginning, Foxy was far too clever a chap not to get his own way in such a matter. Very well liked, he was, and respected too, even then. And so he became Mr. Williams, although, of course, as the years went by and the younger animals grew up, only one here and there ever heard the reason for it."

The animals were strangely quiet. One by one they left their chairs, thanked Brock for his hospitality and for his story, and left for their own homes. Brock was left at last at the door with Popghose, and as he helped him into his coat and tucked his muffler down at the back, he said, "It's getting colder, I think. There'll be a frost in the morning."

10

The Restoration

BROCK was a bit worried. He stood at his table the
following morning, examining the contents of the
shoebox on the lid of which, as we already know, was
scrawled the word EUREKA. It contained the now rather
tangled forms of seven pairs of spectacles, and it was the
smallness of the number that was the cause of Brock's
perplexity. Only seven pairs. Brock reasoned, sensibly
enough, that these seven pairs must have been the last
batch to be tested by the owl. At least three nights had
been spent on the trials, and it had been arranged that
any rejected spectacles should be collected by the messen-
gers when they delivered fresh ones. Assuming that seven
pairs represented one night's rejects, where then were
the rejects of the two previous nights?

He knew well enough, from yesterday's meeting with
Corky, that the jackdaws had done nothing in the way of

returning purloined glasses—Corky had as good as admitted it. The missing fourteen pairs or so were . . . well, where? Now, Brock reasoned, the jackdaws' efforts had got them all out of a very awkward situation, and he felt really grateful for all that they had done. Even if self-preservation had been the motive of Corky's cooperation, it was still a fact that the whole community of animals had benefited. But there was no blinking at the fact that jackdaws were irresponsible, and from the knowledge Brock already possessed he realized that they had either kept the rejects for themselves or, what was little better, had just casually dropped them over the countryside. It was perhaps the second idea that worried him most. If the jackdaws had kept the rejects, then that was the end of that. Corky's attitude of the previous day had shown that there would be no further cooperation in that quarter; so the glasses could be thought of as gone for good, and there was no point in worring further. But what if they were littered over the countryside?

"Well, well," muttered Brock, slowly kicking off his slippers and changing into his shoes. "I'll see what Popghose thinks . . . we must return the handkerchiefs, too. I'll go along and see Popghose."

As he strolled away toward weasel's South Western door, he was overtaken by Hare and Mr. Pointz. "Come along with me to Popghose," said Brock to the two animals, "and you can have your handkerchiefs back. . . . It'll save him a walk, you know, and there'll be a lot to do, one way and another."

They found Popghose bending over the little rustic bench he had arranged at the entrance of the tunnel. With the kit bag half emptied, he was engaged in searching the corners of handkerchiefs for initials and laundry

marks, and had several neat piles arranged before him
on the seat. "Goody, goody," said Popghose, smiling up
at them. "You couldn't have come at a better time to give
me a hand. Initials and laundry marks it is. Unmarked
ones in that pile, O.K.?"

It did not take them long, working at it together, and
toward the end of the task, Popghose disappeared and returned with a jug and glasses. As he poured out the cider
for them, he said to Brock, "Do you know, Mel, I think
we ought to have more spectacles—I mean returned ones,
of course. I don't mean we ought to start all over again,"
he added, laughing.

"Just what I came to see you about, old chap," said
Brock.

They found they had both been considering the same
problems and Popghose said, "Well, look, what about
this? We've got to take back all these hankies, haven't
we? Well, as we go around we'll make each animal we
see responsible for searching his own area. How's that?
Any glasses they find they must return to you, say, as
soon as they find 'em."

Mr. Pointz wondered whether a reward might not be
paid, per pair.

"No, no by Golly, it couldn't," said Popghose. "When
I think of all the trouble some of us have been to—
work, worry and expense unstinted—and how others that
I could mention just sit back and take it all for granted,
with never an offer to run an errand, or anything . . ."

"I'm sorry, Popghose," said Mr. Pointz, "I didn't think
of it like that. Of course you're right. No rewards. No
rewards. Although I was thinking mostly of the youngsters, playing, you know. They might easily come across
the things and know nothing about them . . . not even

know what they are. A jar of hard candy, to be sure, was all I was thinking of. But no, no rewards.''

"Sorry, Hedgy," said Popghose, "there I go again, snapping people's heads off. Your idea is a very good one, and we'll do it. Nothing more likely to work. I'm sorry about catching you up like that. Let me fill your glass.''

"That's all right, Popghose," said Mr. Pointz. "There's no offense . . . I don't mind in the least. I'm not very clever at explaining quickly, you know, and I put it in a silly way. But it would be a good idea, wouldn't it, Popghose? Just a little candy.''

"Yes, that's fine," said Brock. "I'll see about a jar of candy. Jolly good idea, old chap. But we ought to set off. All the calling and whatnot will take up half the day.''

They divided the handkerchiefs into four piles and each took one, having arranged them by their initials into areas. The unknowns and doubtfuls were to be left at Popghose's, and would have to be called for. And each on his calls could leave instructions about searching for glasses and how to return them to Brock, and how there would be a reward of candy for the youngsters. And so, all being arranged, they stuffed handkerchiefs into every available pocket, finished up the jug of cider, and were just about to set off on yet another round of visits, when a squirrel, badly out of breath with running, came to a stop in front of Brock and said, "For you, Mr. Brock!" and thrust a folded note into his paw.

"Well, what's this, my little fellow?" asked Brock, at the same time unfolding the paper. "Why, it's from old Beak . . . well, would you believe it, he's coming to see us. Says he wants to thank everybody in person. Tonight, too. Well, well, the Hon. Richard back at the Club again! Be like old times. We'll have to call a special meeting . . . but that's easy, for we're all going around on this delivery business. Tell all members there will be a special meeting tonight, at eight, say. Old Beak's not likely to be there before nine or so at the earliest, so we'll say eight. Special meeting at the Club at eight. That all right, you chaps?"

Not only was it accepted as all right, but it was looked forward to with considerable excitement. It was many years since old Beak had been with them. To many even middle-aged members, old Beak was nothing but a long-told tale. Very few indeed had ever seen him at the Club. So when at last eight o'clock came and the chattering voices filled the pleasant old room at Brock's, and the punch was again a-brewing, every succeeding knock brought momentary silence, until the newly arrived proved to be not old Beak, but just another member hurrying into the warmth and fellowship of the Club.

But at half past nine an impressive rat-a-tat-tat announced old Beak himself. He walked slowly into the room, and came up to Brock and took his paw. "Mel,

old fellow, I claim old membership, and the indulgence
of all here. But not indulgence as an old member, no;
indulgence in the name of friendship, if you will all
allow me the privilege of calling you my friends.
Although I asked to be allowed to thank you all in
person for what you have done for me, now I am here,
I am at a loss for words and phrases in which to discharge
my debt. Will you take it that, in some small measure,
my very presence here is an acknowledgment of obligation, and that my being among you is by way of demon-
stration that I am here as your servant, and that you can
call upon me for anything within my power? I thank
you all most sincerely for what you have done for me,
and I am very grateful. Now, if you will be so good as to
admit two little friends of mine who are at this moment
outside with a little cart, you will admit that which will
allow us to drink one another's healths tonight, and I
hope for many nights to come."

The two little friends with their little cart proved to be

two stoats from World's End Wood, and their little cart
was laden with two kegs, and as many bottles as there was
space for. Old Beak removed his outer garment, and
Brock pushed him down into his own chair by the hearth
and drew another chair up alongside him.

"And what will you drink, my dear fellow?" asked
Brock. "I see you've brought some cider with you."

"No, no," said the owl, "that's for the Club . . . for you
all. But I see you still continue the excellent business
of making the Club punch. Give me a glass of that. Many
years since I've tasted that. Many years; and a Club meeting without it would not do at all, eh? What?" Old Beak
pronounced the Club punch as good as ever he remembered it, and better. And he promised to send them over
some pineapple juice that he had maturing in a cask
in his cellar.

The happy fire burned brightly. The apple logs gave
out warmth and a perfume that told of long days in
sunny orchards; the golden glow of candles shed a
benevolent radiance upon all below them impartially,
and the loud chatter and the nods and smiles of the
animals might have been locked away in the heart of a
beholder, had there been one, as the very picture of
content. Perhaps a quarter of an hour had passed. The
buzz of talk and laughter had grown a little louder, when
Brock turned to the Hon. Richard William, who had
brought with him a case of clay pipes, called church-
wardens, and was engaged in charging one of them with
tobacco.

"Now, my dear fellow," said Brock, "there's another
old custom in this Club, if you remember it. Our story-
telling has not died. We had, a night or two ago, a most
remarkable narrative from Popghose here. Most re-

markable. It is many years since these walls heard one
from your lips. I have no doubt that the Club would consider itself very honored to hear a story from you—one
of the old tales, if you like. Let me once again call silence
for a story from the Hon. Richard William de Striges . . .
as I used to in days gone by."

The owl looked at Brock, and with a slow smile met
the inquiring eyes of his friend. "All right, Mel, an-
nounce me for a story. Many years since I've told one
though—bit rusty, you know."

Brock turned and rapped on the table. "Gentlemen,
pray silence. We are to hear this evening's story from the
gentleman on my right, a member of this Club, although
not often with us. Pray silence for the Hon. Richard
William Strix Flammea de Striges."

The owl continued to fill his churchwarden, and he
bent down to the fire to light a spill. "I shall," he said,
straightening himself in his chair, "if you will allow me,
tell you the story of the King, the Hermit, and the Two
Robins. I have been told that this story has a moral; I
have also been told that the moral is extremely difficult
to find. But come, you shall all judge for yourselves. To
the story then, which as I said, is called:

THE STORY OF THE KING, THE HERMIT, AND
THE TWO ROBINS

"Not very far from where my house now stands in
World's End Wood there lived, many years ago, a hermit.
Entering the wood late one evening with the intention of
resting there for the night, something within told him
that he need go no farther to seek a site for his hermitage,
and that he had at last come to the place where he would
spend the rest of his life. He had come to the last place.
And when he awoke in the morning, this was confirmed

in him. The broad day revealed that he had chosen the edge of a little clearing deep within the quiet trees, and he thought about the roof he must now build himself, for there was no cave or other natural shelter there. He ate his last remaining piece of bread and found the spring that was, from then on, to supply him with water, and from this he drank. Seven miles back along the road that had led him to the wood, was the last straggling hamlet through which he had passed on his journey, and having finished his simple meal, he set out to return to it.

"Back at the little village, he sat himself on a bank in the sun, and waited for the first man that he should see that he might speak to him. And when the first man came he said to him, 'God be with you. I need a saw and an ax and a plane, and must borrow them, for I have no money. I am to build an hermitage in the wood yonder. How shall I get them?'

"And the man said to him. 'Wait, I have an ax that I will bring you. The saw and the plane I will borrow for you.'

"And the hermit smiled at him and the man returned the way he had come, and after a little while he came back with the saw and the ax and the plane. He had also brought the hermit a chisel and an auger. 'For,' he said, 'with these your task will be made less troublesome.'

"The hermit then said to the man, 'How will you manage now that you have lent me these tools?'

"And the man replied, 'God rest you. We shall manage.'

"And so the hermit wrapped all the tools in his cloak, and swung them over his shoulder and returned to the place where he must build. And the birds and the animals that lived there would hear the hermit sawing and planing and singing as he worked. Day by day the simple little house that he was building grew nearer to completion, and on one side and in the middle of the wall he made a door, and on the wall next to it facing the clearing and the sun that climbed the high trees, he cut a hole for the sun to enter. He also made a shutter for this hole, hung like a door on the outside of the wall, so that he could close it at night and keep the cold wind from entering his house.

"When all was finished, he cleaned all the tools and wrapped them up again in his cloak, and returned them to the man in the village. 'God rest you,' he said, 'I have made my house, and brought you once again your own. God give you good use of them.' And it was said afterward that the saw and the ax kept their edge without blunting, as did also the chisel and the plane and the auger. And the hermit lived in the house that he had built, and the birds and animals walked with him and flew about him, and had no fear. When he opened the wind shutter the birds would fly in to share his bread, or if he had no bread they would rest on the edge of his plate and drink from the pottage of herbs that he gathered in the clearing. And the years came and went, and the generations of birds and animals came and went with the years, and the hermit lived in his house and at peace.

"It so happened that the king of all these parts went on a journey, and the road he had to travel lay through the wood where the hermit lived. Although proud and arrogant and a king, there was still much humanity left in him, and he went into the clearing by himself to see the hermit. And when they had spoken of all that they could to one another, and the king rose up from the hermit's stool on which he had been sitting, he said, 'And what boon shall I give you, Hermit? What gift or rich thing shall I leave you that you may remember this visit?'

" 'But what can you give me?' asked the hermit. 'I want for nothing.'

" 'Let me build an abbey here, for you,' said the king, 'or at least a stone house, with chairs and so on, and books . . . surely it would be good to have books?'

" 'No,' said the hermit, 'I no longer need books. God reward you according to the purity of your intention . . . but I want for nothing.'

"But it is very difficult for kings to understand simple things, and this king was both amused and perhaps a little angry with the hermit who had accepted him as a man but not as a creature of power, and he strode out into the clearing and through the wood to call up his important men. 'Find,' he said 'something to do to the hermit's house, that it may be improved and not a disgrace to us and a byword that we left it as we found it.'

"The important men looked at the simple house of the hermit, and their spokesman said, 'Your Majesty, the house has no glass window. It has a shutter against the wind only. Even a hermit must be grateful for a glass window.'

"And the king smiled again and said. 'Make it. But make it so that it opens like a shutter, and hangs in the window hole, and then the hermit will find that he has no loss but a gain. For all that he had before will be as before, but in addition he will have light without wind when he so desires.'

"They made the glass window and hung it so that it opened, and it swung in the window hole and inside the

wind shutter. And before they went away the king said,
'See, I have spoiled nothing. But I have given you one
new thing, and a good one.'

"And the hermit answered and said, 'The intention
will be rewarded according to the virtue in it. Go in
peace.'

"When he arose the following morning, the hermit
went, as was his custom, and threw back the wind shutter
that the sun and the birds might enter his house. And
seeing it was now open two robins left the edge of the
clearing flying straight for the hermit's window that they
might share his morning meal. The hermit had already
forgotten the glass, and the robins knew nothing of it,
nor could they have understood it had they known.
And so it fell out that one of them was killed outright
as he hit the glass, but his brother escaped death, and
although he fell to the ground beneath the window he
eventually recovered conciousness, and with returning
strength he flew back the way he had come, and was able
to tell of the disaster that had overtaken his brother.
The assembled birds listened in silence to his story, and
did not believe it to be true. The window was known to
them all. All had flown through it and all at various
times had shared the simple meals of the hermit, and
the robin was accused of killing his brother. In vain he
pleaded his guiltlessness. The sensation of flying into
solid air that he tried so hard to describe was outside
their comprehension, and he was thrown into prison to
await his trial.

"But even in the primitive time of which I speak,
justice was held desirable, and the reign of law already
established. Prejudged although he was, he was allowed
counsel, and an older bird whose opinion was respected

was allowed to discuss the thing with him, and put the
little that could be said in his favor before the court.
This bird heard the story once again. How the air had
seemingly coagulated at the opening of the window, the
the jolt of the sudden stopping, and the consequent fall.

"And this bird said, 'Why not?' Even though it has
never happened before, might it not happen now? Water
turned into ice. Might not a similar thing happen to air?
And so he said at the trial that he was convinced of the
innocence of the accused. True, solid air was not known
to them before, but all things must have a beginning,
and long years had made him understand that the world
changed. Water changed into ice. But not everywhere.
In the South, once they had flown over the great hills,
there was no ice. Perhaps solid air came to them from
the North, and like the ice that it resembled could
dissolve itself into plain air again. An element of doubt
crept in among the little creatures. Might this not be
so? The world was mysterious and the wisest of them
knew very little.

"And then spoke the prosecution. Solid air! Who,
except the accused, had ever encountered it? What
rubbish to talk so. What wickedness. Was not the crime
itself bad enough, that blasphemy had to be called in to
enrich it? To accuse the gods of altering the air! How
should birds exist if the very element in which they had
their being was liable to change and clog them—to
solidify with suddenness and bring them to death. It
was impossible. It was nonsense. The weak dribbling of a
foolish brain that invented impossibilities to avoid the
consequences of crime. 'If this thing can be,' he
thundered, 'then we are all undone. Nature confounds
herself. Think well before you let this extravagance in-

fluence you. The creature is guilty.'

"The debate raged. Birds were uncertain and divided in their opinion, but in the end they said, 'We do not know. Let us put the thing to the proof.'

"But there arose yet a third school of opinion. There was no killing. There was no solid air. The gods destroyed the unrighteous, and the gods alone knew who they were. When the time came, and the patience of the gods was exhausted, they stretched forth their finger and pointed, and the wicked died. It was so from all time, and none could escape. What proof was there of a killing? None whatever. The bird had been found with his neck broken, but what sort of proof was that? Was every death a killing? But the gods were just, if incomprehensible. They alone knew. They alone pointed a finger and the wicked died.

"The debate continued. But gradually what had been the small murmur of a few grew in volume and insistence: 'Put the thing to the proof!' But this was serious indeed, and the waverers one by one dropped into silence, and a shrugged shoulder. 'Who knows? One might think . . . but that is not to be certain.' And so they dropped away. But the fanatical held on. The proof would be their vindication, and a trial was to be arranged.

"The day dawned in beautiful gray light. Slowly the mists dissolved and each dewdrop held a tiny sun, to make living light in the strips of emerald between stretched shadows of the trees around the clearing. The hermit awoke to the beams as they streamed in on him through the cracks of his house, and he got up from the heap of bracken that was his sufficient bed and threw open his door. His every movement was a rejoicing in the new day's light, and he went outside to his window shutter and flung it back. He did not return immediately to his room, for he went into the trees to get sticks for his fire, and so he neither saw nor heard the thud as the bird for the prosecution dropped to the ground after impact with the glass of the inner window. And as the flutter of rescuing birds sought him, and carried the little body back to the edge of the wood, the words '. . . solid air, indeed . . . utter nonsense . . .' were the last he spoke.

"Returning with his sticks, the hermit stood in uncertainty within his threshold. What was wrong with the light? With a smile and a little shake of his head he pushed outward the great king's present, and had scarcely turned his back to the window when a robin alighted upon his table in front of him.

" 'Ah, you're early this morning. Look . . . I have only just returned with my sticks. But you shall have bread.'

"The robin, however, did not wait for the crumbs. He was triumphant. He had vindicated the gods who pointed their finger, and he flew back in glory to the edge of the wood and to the few faithful."

As the owl ended his story, it was as though he had drawn a curtain of silence into the now deeply shadowed room. Two of the candles had already flickered into darkness, and the unreplenished fire glowed richly but without flame. For a few moments it was as though all life and movement was suspended by the very ending of his voice, but one by one the little animals moved in their chairs, but softly, as though each was still within the story and could only emerge slowly and by stealth. Popghose stretched himself and stood up, and looked down at the owl now silent in his chair. "What a most beautiful story . . . most beautiful. But I do not understand all of it."

The owl looked up and smiled at him. "Perhaps it cannot be fully understood," he said. "Perhaps that's the secret of it."

And Brock said, "Yes, perhaps that was, after all, the whole point of it."

WILLIAM SMALLBONE, who is now about to be introduced to the reader and whose name would have been even more descriptive of his appearance had it been curtailed by the last four letters, was standing in his house before a looking glass, in the passage that he called The Hall, making himself neat and tidy. For neatness he was combing his sparse gray hair fanwise across his small head, and the tidying would follow when, with his cap arranged to avoid messing his hair, he would carefully tuck the top of his ears under the cap band. For unlike the rest of his small person, his ears, hands and feet were unnecessarily large. There was nothing but a foot of wall between the looking glass and the street, except the front door, and this being now opened, William Smallbone let himself out into the thoroughfare.

He had not far to go. Although it is perhaps unnecessary for the purposes of my story, I cannot refrain from informing the reader that William Smallbone had at one time been master of his own business. He had, with the assistance of his wife, Gladys, sold provisions retail, for consumption by domestic pets . . . or to put it more bluntly, he had been a cats'-meat man. His trade had dwindled and almost disappeared under the pressure from the larger enterprise of modern business, and the branded and labeled can, extensively advertised in the daily newspapers, had finally finished him. At the time of which I speak, his father, although happily still alive, was in rapidly failing health, and his continued employment at St. Matthew and St. Aloysius as a sexton and general handyman was a matter of debate. Knowing this to be so, William waylaid the Vicar and asked for the job, representing to that gentleman that his father had suggested it, and assuring him that a very small pension would be sufficient to keep the old man happy. These artful doings were successful. William Smallbone obtained the post of sexton and general handyman, and it is in this capacity that we have already found him leaving his home, and about to walk the short distance that separated him from the church, and to enter the west porch of that imposing building.

Mr. Smallbone was, by nature, a man easily irritated. The season, as the attentive reader knows, was that of early autumn, and leaves, assisted by a cutting east wind, were already scurrying into hiding and looking for places in which to spend the winter. Looked at professionally, Mr. Smallbone regarded leaves with a particular hatred as the chief cause of his endless labor, and as he approached the church and watched the eddying gusts of wind redistribute the piles he had not yet been able to burn, his heart grew black within him. Rounds of confetti, hitherto lodged safely in crevices of the stonework, leaped out to join the leaves, and although only present in small numbers they served to remind Mr. Smallbone of how he loathed confetti and the sweeping of it. In addition to all this, he had a gumboil.

Entering the porch, by unlocking the outer iron gate that closed it, his eyes, stinging a little from grit carried by the wind, fell upon an object resting upon the right-hand stone seat within. It appeared to be a cardboard box, and by certain lettering suggested that it had once contained shoes. Long experience of parcels left in the porch had convinced Mr. Smallbone that they were never worth the undoing. Indeed, most of them, he knew, were best left undone. In a transport of fury Mr. Smallbone leapt onto the seat and dealt the box a vigorous kick, straightaway following up the action by jumping upon it as it lay on the flagstones. His next kick was a particularly good one, for the box rose a little into the air, left the porch, struck a plane tree bordering the flagged path, and landed with a tinkling sound at the feet of the Rev. Hugh Davidson-Davidson, who at that very moment had turned into the churchyard.

The reverend gentleman was quite as capable of putting two and two together as any man, and having noticed the rapid retreat of his sexton into the church, smiled to himself, and gave a second glance to the box which lay at his feet. The word EUREKA leered at him from the battered top, and what appeared to be the earpiece of a pair of tortoiseshell glasses projected drunkenly from a rent in its side. You may picture the clergyman as though frozen in a half-bent position as, with the smile slowly leaving his pleasant face, he extended a hand toward the box. He lifted it by the soiled and knotted string and carried it slowly into the church. His thoughts were a turmoil, but as he approached the vestry he called out loudly, in the direction where he imagined his sexton to be, "Smallbone . . . be good enough to attend me in the vestry, will you?"

Mr. Smallbone, in no way conscious of the havoc he had caused or the certainty of unemployment into which his irritation had led him, entered the vestry to find his

employer emptying the contents of the box onto the green
baize of the table. The tinkling mass of crushed glass
and wire, tortoiseshell and plastic, settled down and
stared at them, and they stared at one another.

"Why on earth were you so foolish . . . so criminal
. . . so . . . so . . . wanton as to destroy them?" asked the
Rev. Hugh of his astonished sexton. "Here, by some
miracle, were the lost spectacles of half the parish . . .
and see what you have done! Have you gone mad?"

There is seldom any answer to this sort of question. To
have told the clergyman of the east wind, the leaves, the
grit and the gumboil would have required a man of more
imagination than William Smallbone. He just said that
he didn't know what the box contained.

"But you might have examined it! You didn't have
to destroy it without looking, did you? Wanton destruction . . . just wanton destruction. For heaven's sake, get
out of my sight. What on earth the parish will say, I don't
know. . . . I Do Not Know!"

The sexton vanished on the instant. Whether with the idea of protecting Mr. Smallbone from the fury of the parish, or whether from some secret purpose of his own, we shall never know, but the Rev. Hugh swept the littered remains of the spectacles back into the cardboard box, walked quickly back into the body of his church, and removed the lid of the coke stove. The red-hot coals quietly received the offering, and never afterward mentioned the matter. Neither did the Rev. Hugh. Nor for that matter did Mr. Smallbone.

That gentleman is once again in the cats'-meat line, but in a very small way, with a small handcart, and an almost smaller round. The mystery of the vanished glasses still makes a topic of conversation in the little village, and there are almost as many theories to account for their disappearance as there are people who lost them. Only the excellent bifocals once the property of Mr. Wooley, the schoolmaster, survived. And, had he known it, they could have been seen any evening, mounted upon the high and dignified nose of the owl, the Hon. Richard William Strix Flammea de Striges, as he silently quartered the fields and verges in search of his legitimate prey.

WILL NICKLESS, who has both written OWLGLASS and done the illustrations for it, lives with his wife and two daughters in Sussex, England. He has made drawings for numerous books and magazines, including the one of himself, above. Of himself, he says that he is constantly reminded of the need for continual awareness that things are by no means what they seem to be.

PRINTED
IN
U. S. A.

20